Salty Waters

A new career as a glamour model was Tracy Ashford's way of escape from the dullness of the seaside town where she lived: but the local worthies didn't like it, and it cost her her title as a local beauty queen—and her life.

It was Detective-Inspector Alec Stainton's misfortune to be holidaying in the town the day Tracy died. Instead of sunning himself on the sands he finds himself seeing a side of the town which never appeared in the tourist brochures.

The dead girl's picture is before him in more ways than one as he follows her among the seaside crowds and through the shadows of London clubland to her final rendezvous with her killer.

STEPHEN MURRAY

Salty Waters

COLLINS, 8 GRAFTON STREET, LONDON W1

William Collins Sons & Co. Ltd
London · Glasgow · Sydney · Auckland
Toronto · Johannesburg

First published 1988
© Stephen Murray 1988

British Library Cataloguing in Publication Data

Murray, Stephen
 Salty waters.—(Crime Club)
 I. Title
 823'.914[F]   PR6063.U7

 ISBN 0 00 232187 4

Photoset in Linotron Baskerville by
Rowland Phototypesetting Ltd
Bury St Edmunds, Suffolk
Printed in Great Britain by
William Collins Sons & Co. Ltd, Glasgow

CHAPTER 1

Alec Stainton sat on the beach and stared out to sea. The sun shone whitely in a deep blue sky. Some yards away little wavelets slapped playfully at the even sand, while further out the sea's surface swelled and sank in hypnotic rhythm. It was the third successive day that Alec had sat in this spot, and each had been hotter and more peaceable than the last.

'Blast,' said Alec audibly. A passing toddler, startled, gave him a slow, wide-eyed look and began to run with jerking steps towards parents and ice-cream. 'Blast,' said Alec again, but this time under his breath.

'You do look ever so cross,' said a voice behind him. 'We've been watching you. And you were here yesterday, and you looked ever so cross yesterday as well. Have you been waiting for someone?'

Turning his head, Alec saw a pair of bare, sandy feet with cramped toes; and calves, a little red but beginning to shade into a more desirable tan. He craned his head and followed the legs up to an exiguous bikini bottom strained perilously over lean, wide hips. He shaded his eyes with his hand. Above the hips was a pale stomach, and above the stomach, he was rather relieved to see, a halter top to match the bikini bottom, equally exiguous and also rather strained. Above all this he finally saw a face. The sun, high over the sea, showed him that it was a pleasant face, and it wore an expression compounded equally of friendly concern and fear of rebuff.

'I'm not waiting for anyone,' he said. 'I'm sorry I looked cross.'

'Oh. Because it's been so lovely that we couldn't see why you should be so fed up.'

The girl nodded back up the beach and Alec saw a little pile of belongings, a vacated towel, and a recumbent figure. 'My friend,' the girl said. 'Heather.' She waited, then, as he didn't ask, volunteered, 'I'm Cathy. Heather said we should leave you be, but when we saw you here again today I thought that was mean.'

'That's very kind of you,' Alec said. 'I'm sorry I looked so fierce. You're right, it is a lovely day.'

'Come over and join us,' Cathy offered tentatively. 'That is, if you'd like to. Don't worry,' she added quickly, 'we're not trying to disturb you if you'd rather be on your own. Only it seems a shame to be miserable when you're on holiday.'

Alec pictured the wide hips softened with the passing of the years, the flat stomach blurred, the neat waist thickened, and realized that the expression of motherly concern would be just the same then as it was now, on the beach, in the gaudy bikini. 'All right,' he said, surprising himself, 'I'll join you.'

'Heather said you wouldn't come,' Cathy confided as he gathered up his things and followed her across the sand. 'She thought I was trying to . . . you know . . . interfere too much. Or pick you up. But I never pick men up on the beach. Or anywhere else,' she added artlessly.

'This is Heather. I don't know your name,' Cathy said shyly, 'so I can't introduce you.'

Heather rolled over on her towel and sat up. She was of Cathy's age, somewhere just over twenty, Alec guessed, dark, where the other girl was fair, with a serious, attractive face. Youth, and vitality, and health, only a little paled from working too much indoors, shone in their bodies and as he introduced himself and set out his towel beside theirs Alec resigned himself to enjoying the day rather more than he had anticipated.

Enjoyment had hardly been Alec's aim in arranging the holiday. Disappointed in his expectation that Jayne Simmonds would share the holiday with him, preparatory to sharing his flat, Alec had snubbed her with unmerciful and, he now felt miserably, unforgivable cruelty. He had tried to resume his affair with a previous girlfriend, only to be told coolly that she had 'moved beyond him'. This evidence of his worthlessness, coupled with the depression which always seemed to accompany the ending of a case, had led him into a protracted and unpleasant fit of the sulks which he recalled with shame and embarrassment. He would have done without a holiday altogether if he could. As it was, he had delivered himself with deliberate perversity to the utterly conventional—a fortnight at a seaside boarding-house.

But the boarding-houses he remembered from childhood had been turned into self-catering apartments, and the dour and regimental landladies were living out their days in Spanish villas and Cheltenham nursing homes. In the end he had found a small hotel where he thought he might, with care, be suitably inconvenienced, but he was hard put to find the lineaments of the traditional landlady in the gentle and indulgent spinsters who ran it.

Three days into his fortnight, Alec found to his chagrin that the relaxation, the freedom from responsibility and the famed ozone had improved his temper despite himself. But then this morning a passing couple giggled and squeezed hands and somewhere in their mutual delight was a gesture, a mannerism, a turn of the head which brought Jayne Simmonds back to him once more, and the thought of what he had thrown away had cast him again into dejection.

'I'm afraid we're forcing our company on you when you'd rather be on your own.' Heather's voice, quiet and resonant, recalled him to the present. She watched him straightforwardly as she waited for his reply.

'I've been on my own quite as much as is good for me,' he said lightly. 'You were quite right to take me to task.'

'You must thank Cathy for that.'

'Yes, it was my idea,' Cathy said. 'I'm so glad you aren't

offended. It might have seemed an awful cheek. We've got an apartment,' she continued chattily. 'It's really very pleasant. We weren't sure about staying in England this year. Usually we've been abroad. You must come over and see us. Can you do that? Why don't you come for a meal?'

Alec thought of the accommodating Miss Hanson and Miss Helston at the hotel. 'I expect I could. If you really want me to come.'

'Oh yes,' Cathy said happily. 'Don't we, Heth? It'll be nice to have someone to cook for besides ourselves. We could make it a little party.'

They swam, and lazed, and chatted, and Alec's wellbeing returned. Perhaps, he mused, he had seen too much of police business in these last few years—too much of grubbiness, betrayed affection, callous cynicism, in criminals and in the Force alike. The simple happiness of Cathy, and the quieter content of Heather, matched the blue sky and the dazzling sun and the rippling waves teasing the sand and there could be, he thought, worse ways of spending a holiday after all.

Later in the day they parted, for the girls had some shopping to do and Alec felt it only polite to leave them to themselves for the little ritual of changing on the beach. Contentedly he strolled along the margin of the sand, swinging the bag containing his things. Glittering in the distance, the famous pier stretched its tracery finger out over the sea. White pavilions flashed and sparkled in the sun and tiny breakers frothed round the iron legs. Then, between himself and the pier, Alec suddenly noticed a crowd gathering, sucking people from their places on the beach as a magnet sucks iron filings. Some of the tiny figures were running, and Alec wondered what could be so compelling on such a hot day. A beach mission? Punch and Judy? So close to the sea's edge?

'Hey, watch out!' An injured cry reminded him to watch where he was treading and he looked down at the trail of havoc he had wrought across a sophisticated irrigation system. A ten-year-old, offended, regarded him accusingly.

'Sorry,' Alec said, and made himself pause and smile to show that he meant it before passing on.

A tinny wail drifted across the foreshore, and up on the esplanade Alec caught the flashing of a blue light, feeble in the bright sun. The police car drew up level with the gathering crowd and Alec shrugged and turned away to climb the beach towards the road. If it was police business then he was definitely not going to get involved.

Stopping at the sea-wall to pull on his jeans and shoes and slip a T-shirt over his head, Alec crossed the road and plunged into the web of alleyways which lay behind the seafront hotels, bearing steadily inland.

In the diminutive foyer of the Logan Hotel tea was being served to such of the residents as were about. Alec slipped into the cloakroom to leave his bag and run a comb through his hair before returning to one of the wicker chairs. Miss Helston, coming into the foyer with a pot of tea for the Captain, flashed him a little smile and reappeared in a very few minutes with tea in a little brown pot, sandwiches and delicate cakes, all of which she placed on one of the tables within Alec's reach. He sat back and looked about him with pleasure. The wicker chairs, the elephant's foot umbrella stand, the etched glass doors to the lobby, even the very people here, were so delightfully of a piece as to be bizarre. They were out of their time. In an earlier age they might have been found in a hundred places out of all the wide red expanses of the globe where the British administered their own vision of civilization. In Singapore, in Rangoon, in Simla and Cairo this way of life might be no more. Here in the Logan Hotel it had never died.

'Pass the sugar,' the Captain said gruffly. Alec, who suspected that the captaincy as much as the gruffness was assumed for effect, leant across obligingly. Concentrating, the Captain spooned three sugars deliberately into his tea, which was milkless. Alec watched the ritual, entranced.

'Hear they've fished a stiff out of the water,' the Captain offered abruptly.

'Oh?'

'Absolutely.'

'When?'

'This afternoon.'

'There was a crowd on the beach as I came past.'

'That's it.'

How on earth, Alec wondered, could the Captain have such an up-to-date intelligence system? The news, however, was upstaged. Old Miss Wynne-Andrews, shackled with rugs to her chair, caught the Captain's barking tones and leant perilously towards them.

'A young woman,' she said, in a penetrating undertone. 'Dead. Drowned.'

'I suppose she would be, if they pulled her out of the water,' Alec volunteered foolishly. The Captain looked at him fiercely. Miss Wynne-Andrews leant back in her chair. Then she seemed to remember the most important, the most piquant, fact and leant slowly forward till Alec was sure he heard her back creak. With an impassive face which dared him to react she uttered one damning word.

'Naked.'

'Uh? What?' The Captain, caught off guard, jerked in his chair and spilt crumbs of sandwich on to the carpet.

'Naked,' repeated Miss Wynne-Andrews with inexorable satisfaction. 'The girl. Naked. When they pulled her out.'

'Good Lord! Really? Good gracious me.'

Gratified, Miss Wynne-Andrews allowed herself to resume her former position.

'Naked,' she said again to herself, and the grim head nodded slowly, twice.

Silence descended on the foyer again, broken only by discreet munching. No wonder there had been a crowd on the beach, Alec thought cynically. If the poor girl had been fished from the waves without a stitch on, the fact that she was dead would be of secondary importance for the spectators. Oh, well, bang went the resort's reputation as the safest bathing beach in the south.

Cathy and Heather had pressed their invitation for that very evening, but Alec, shy of such youthful forthrightness, had promised only to meet them on the beach the next day. They were pleasant, easy company, and it was flattering to be in demand. He had little doubt that, if he chose, their friendship could go much further, certainly on a physical level. But he had passed the stage at which all he wanted to do was grasp love as recompense, or revenge, for his failure with Jayne, and the urgency of a holiday romance held little intrinsic appeal. He could take it or leave it.

Instead, he savoured the Logan Hotel, smiled at its residents and, after a better meal than any boarding-house he could recall had ever produced, strolled out in the evening air to gaze in shop windows, saunter among the alleys and antique shops, and lean against the railings on the seafront watching the narrow line of surf glimmering in the dusk as the waves receded.

It was late when Alec returned to the Logan Hotel, and the lobby was lit only by a single light, spilling out to the pavement below. Within, the wicker chairs, the rubber plant, the elephant's foot loomed dimly in the shadows as Alec crossed to take his key from the rack. As he reached for it, a bulkier shadow disengaged itself from the recesses of the foyer with a suddenness which made him jump.

'Mr Stainton?'

'That's right,' Alec said briefly, seeing a solid, no longer young police constable, uniformed, looking none too pleased at being kept waiting.

'You must come with me, sir, if you please. To the station.'

'Oh yes?' Alec said, irritated at the constable's manner. 'May I ask why?'

'You'll find out when we get there. Now, if you please, sir.'

It was plain why this graceless, unsubtle man had stayed so long a constable. But perhaps, thought Alec with remorseless sympathy, I should be as rude if I were still a constable at fifty. Nevertheless, he was sufficiently piqued to wish the man to be discomforted in his officiousness.

'I'm afraid I'd rather go to bed. All right? So you've waited to no purpose. I'll call at the station first thing.'

'Now you look here,' the policeman began, and the grudging 'sir' had disappeared altogether, 'we've better things to do in this town than waste our time with troublemakers. Where you come from you may get away with it but if you don't come along with me, now, then it might well be a case of wasting police time, or obstructing the police in the execution of their duty.'

'Rubbish,' said Alec angrily. 'If you've got a reason for asking me to come with you, you jolly well out with it and I'll see if I think it's a good one. Otherwise, I'll call in the morning.'

He turned away to the stairs, irritated that even such a small task should be so ham-fistedly carried out. To his astonishment, no sooner had he turned his back than his arm was seized and twisted into a straight arm lock which had considerably more pain in it than was necessary, and the big constable marched him purposefully to the door, scrabbling as best he could at the same time for his personal radio. They blundered through the doors in a macabre parody of a tango and stumbled down the steps, and Alec seriously feared he would end up on the pavement with the bulky constable on top of him. The policeman was still talking into his radio and somewhere in the distance a siren began to wail. Alec glanced up instinctively at the blank windows of the Logan Hotel's upper floors, and repented of his awkwardness. He didn't begrudge the Captain and Miss Wynne-Andrews the scandal of the arrest of one of the guests, but it was poor return for the kindness of Miss Helston and Miss Hanson. At least the drama would be played out on the pavement, and not in the lobby itself.

'All right,' he said curtly, 'I'll come with you. For heaven's sake get them to turn that siren off, and let go of my arm.'

'Shut up.' Alec felt his arm given a fresh wrench, and fumed at his impotence. 'Look,' he said, 'didn't they tell you I'm in the Force?'

It hardly sounded plausible, even to him, and certainly made no impression on the constable, who said nothing. The siren was much closer now, and the glare of headlights and a flashing blue light were reflected off the houses on the other side of the square as the car swept round the corner. It squealed to a halt diagonally across the road. Two men leapt out, leaving the doors gaping.

'Now then,' one said to Alec firmly, but Alec noted that he shot no very confident glance at Alec's captor.

'This isn't the chap the boss sent you to bring in? We thought you'd been bounced by a villain.'

'This is the one. Young Lord Muck, decided he didn't want to come and started to resist. I had to put a lock on him for my own defence.'

Alec sighed at the blatant lie. The second man from the car had come round now and looked at Alec doubtfully. Alec was conscious of the indignity of his position.

'Can we have your name, sir?'

'Stainton,' Alec said heavily. 'Detective-Inspector. I would show you my warrant card if I could reach it.'

The newcomers looked awkward. 'I think the boss was hoping he could have a word with you, sir. About this drowning on the beach. Bernard here was sent to ask if you'd call round.'

Bernard reluctantly eased his grip on Alec's arm. He felt, rightly, that he'd been made a fool of, and resented it.

'If you could just show us your warrant card, sir?'

Alec fished it out, and the young constable barely glanced at it. It was recognizable enough. Bernard said nothing.

Alec asked the policemen to wait and reluctantly returned to the foyer and called Miss Helston. It was not quite midnight, and she was still up, waiting to lock up. Alec persuaded her to let him have a key, offering his warrant card in explanation, for he had booked his holiday, of course, as plain 'Mr'. On an impulse, he asked her to say nothing of who he was to the other residents.

'I'm sorry about all this,' he said.

'We were a little anxious, for of course we knew that that police constable was waiting for you. I'm afraid some of the residents knew it, too.'

'Let them think what they like. The idea of one of their fellow guests being hauled off to gaol will brighten their day. I'll be back, though, and I'll find a way of ensuring they know a mistake had been made. I shouldn't like them to think this is the sort of hotel that criminals come to.'

'That's so kind of you. Reputation does mean so much to a hotel like this, you know. I may say that we ourselves were quite sure there was nothing amiss. It is quite clear that you are not that sort of person.'

Alec, a little burdened by this reassurance, thanked her and rejoined his captors. The older constable, Bernard, had left to continue his beat, in high dudgeon, and the two younger men were subdued as they drove Alec sedately enough to the town's main police station, in the deserted central square.

Inside, Alec was shown into the office of a trim uniformed inspector of forty or so, who looked up sharply and gave Alec a steady, if not unfriendly, scrutiny as he gestured him to a chair.

'Farmer,' he said by way of introduction. Alec nodded.

'Now,' Inspector Farmer went on, 'I don't know if you've heard, but we had a drowning here this afternoon. That's very regrettable, especially if you're a councillor on the

tourism sub-committee. Personally, I think it regrettable
enough anyway.'

Alec looked politely interested, wondering where he came
in. He was not inclined to be involved, and didn't see why
he should be. Inspector Farmer nodded, as if aware of Alec's
thoughts.

'Unfortunately, it's not totally straightforward—that is,
it may not be. And,' he added heavily, 'it coincides with a
little bit of trouble of our own. You know our DI, Henryson?'

Alec nodded. 'Not well,' he said. 'We've met, of course.'

'Well, he's got himself into hot water.' Farmer looked
annoyed. 'He may, and I say may, have been fiddling his
expense sheet. If he has, he needs his head examining. You
know as well as I do that it's the one crime they really
get worked up about in this Force. Seducing the Chief
Constable's daughter is nothing beside it. Consequence, he's
been suspended on full pay, pending an investigation. As
from yesterday.' The Inspector stared at his desk, disgusted,
as he contemplated his colleague's folly.

Alec waited, knowing now what he was going to hear.

Farmer raised his eyes to Alec's with grim sympathy.
'This evening, when it looked as if this drowning was going
to be more complicated than we thought, I rang County
HQ. You see, Henryson's sergeant has been deputizing for
him since yesterday. We don't see much spectacular crime
down here, thank heaven, so there's not much a sergeant
can't deal with. But if it's murder, that's a different question
altogether.'

'Murder,' Alec echoed. 'It is, is it?'

'It may be. I'll tell you why in a moment. Anyway, you
know what I'm going to say. County ran round in circles
for an hour or two wondering who to draft down here, then
some bright spark cottoned on to your contact address and
the upshot was that your Super decided we ought to haul
you in. He seems to think you didn't do too badly last time
he used you on a murder. He's going to ring you here

tomorrow to speak to you and make it formal, but meanwhile he told me to haul you in straight away so that you could get to work. I don't think he's giving you much option.'

'Bang goes my holiday, then,' Alec said wryly.

'I'm afraid so.'

'You're not doing your best to give me happy memories of this place, are you?'

'Bernard's an oaf,' the Inspector said savagely. Alec forbore to suggest that a fuller briefing might have encouraged Bernard to be more delicate.

'OK,' he said heavily. 'Let me have what you've got so far.'

'Good,' said Farmer briskly. He pressed a button on his desk and a constable appeared. Farmer ordered coffee and asked them to run up some sandwiches. He himself looked as if he was freshly on duty. Alec, by contrast, felt tired and shabby. He forced his mind to turn more keenly.

'Why do we think it might not be a straightforward drowning?' Farmer asked rhetorically. 'One, because we found no clothes. Two, because of who she is.'

'You identified her, then?' Alec asked. 'Although she was naked?'

Farmer looked at him. 'In the circumstances, that was quite ironic. She's Tracy Ashford. Up to last month, Miss Southern Belle of the year.'

'Up to last month?'

'She was stripped of her title,' said the Inspector with grim amusement, 'stripped being an entirely appropriate word in this case. For posing nude in a national newspaper. This is a very moral little town, Mr Stainton.'

CHAPTER 2

Cathy and Heather greeted the new day with raised spirits. Until yesterday they had been feeling that though holidaying in Britain was pleasant enough, it was a little on the dull side. In Crete or Corfu there would have been beach discos and busy cafés, and all the interest of the unfamiliar: although, to be sure, increasing familiarity had been a factor in their decision to stay at home this year. Here they had all the sun, all the sand and swimming they could wish for, but you did miss a certain excitement, a certain sense of danger and of the possibility of breaking normal rules. Even the young men, of which there were few enough, in all conscience, were tediously polite and unpushy. If only they even spoke a different language.

Alec's presence on the beach had been one of the few touches of mystery, and now that friendship had begun between them, things were looking happier. He was interestingly enigmatic, Cathy thought. You fancied you were swapping gossip about each other quite freely, only to find at the end of the conversation that though you had told him plenty about yourself, you knew no more of him than you did at the start. There wouldn't be any real mystery to him, of course, just as there was no real romance in the Manuels and Angelos of previous holidays, but you had to have your little illusions, or where were you? All the same, it was a shame there was only one of him, she thought meditatively, looking across to Heather stuffing things into a bag, because it had been plain that he was more interested in Heth than in herself. All the best men were, she thought ruefully, while she was left with the ones who simply liked big tits. She hoped he wouldn't let Heth down too roughly . . . but then, you never knew these days, with men. Both girls were on

the pill, because that was only sensible, even if you rarely
—well, hardly ever, really—wanted to let them go that far.
But now, with this awful AIDS, and not knowing where
people had been before . . . after all, if they did it with you,
they did it with others . . . she did hope Heth would be
careful, because however nice he was, it wasn't as if it was
permanent. They were only on holiday.

Heather looked up from her packing, and Cathy changed
her anxious frown for a cheery smile. Heth had her head
screwed on. And there was all today to look forward to.

Down on the beach, the tide was on the way out and there
was plenty of room. They set up camp in their usual spot,
just out of hearing of the funfair and well away from the
public conveniences. Families were pegging out their windbreaks, shaking out their towels. They laid theirs out and
Cathy slipped off her skirt. It wasn't yet quite hot enough
to take her T-shirt off, perhaps, so she reached for the suntan
lotion and began to smooth it into her legs. Really, they
were turning quite a good colour. And, though she said it
herself, there wouldn't be many better pairs of legs on the
beach today than hers and Heth's.

She caught her friend glancing along the beach, trying
not to be too obvious. Alec's spot was still empty. Of course,
it was early still, yet it was just a little unflattering that he
should not have come down as soon as he could. It wasn't
as if they would be difficult to find. She craned her head to
check their position in relation to the beach huts and the
promenade steps, half hoping to see his lean figure striding
towards them through the crowd. Oh well, there was plenty
of time.

In the diminutive police station Alec stared balefully into
the bottom of his paper cup and decided that the coffee was
probably cold. The absent Henryson's office was small and
mean, the desk drawers a muddle of rubber bands and
broken pencils, the top cluttered with senseless executive

knick-knacks around the stained blotter. Dog-eared leave
rosters hung on the wall beside gaudy prints of Constable's
Haywain and *Cornfield* in cheap utility frames. The room
smelt of stale smoke and somebody else's body and Alec
contemplated the hours he would spend pent in it with no
enthusiasm at all.

Opposite the desk, a young man with short hair and an
earnest manner pinned something to the door. Detective-
Sergeant Pringle was efficient, painstaking and thoroughly
conventional. He was also piqued. Two days ago, when
Henryson had been relieved of duty, Pringle had found it
hard to conceal his excitement. The principal had been
struck down and he had been plucked from the chorus line
to take his place. True, there was little in the way of crime
in the town. Nevertheless, Pringle had been given his chance,
and he would make sure he made the most of it.

Then, when he had occupied Henryson's chair for less
than a day, this silly girl had drowned and Inspector Farmer
had gone crying to County with tales of murder. Now, as a
consequence, here was an unknown DI sitting in that very
same chair, and anything Pringle did now would be totally
overlooked in the flurry of what this interloper got up to
over Tracy Ashford.

Pringle pushed the last drawing-pin in viciously and stood
back. Rather crumpled, and with a tear across one arm,
Tracy Ashford pouted cheekily back at him from the cheap
newsprint. Terrific Tracy, said the caption, whom the kill-
joy councillors had stripped of her beauty-queen title. How
dare they? And Tracy, kneeling saucily on the sand of the
photographer's studio, bucket and spade beside her, seemed
to laugh with delight that they could make themselves so
ridiculous. Well, thought Pringle, she wasn't laughing now.

Alec gazed at the tattered pin-up and sucked his teeth.
They had phoned through to the newspaper for glossies of
all the photos that had been taken at the session. They
would have to ask Tracy's parents for a more demure picture

to use for public consumption, but for the time being there
was not much sense to be got out of Mr and Mrs Ashford.
All he had was this one pin-up, rifled from the locker room
where the constables had joked and ogled and then left it,
one among many, to yellow and fade and be torn down at
last to make way for another, more recent, nude.

Not that Tracy was totally nude in the picture, of course.
It was a standard topless pose, with skimpy briefs just visible
in the crease of her hips. Sand speckled her torso and breasts,
stuck, Alec suspected, not by the salt sea but with more
prosaic Copydex. She wore earrings and a necklace, and
bracelets at her wrists, and her hair was swept up on top of
her head and held by a bright grip. The stomach was flat
and muscled and the face, for all its practised cheekiness,
intelligent and even, Alec thought, a trifle wistful. She was,
he learnt, a doctors' receptionist who now hoped to make a
career in modelling. Didn't they all?

At four o'clock that same morning Alec had stood beside
Inspector Farmer at the hospital while a gloomy mortuary
assistant had pulled out the drawer marked Ashford, Tracy.
Alec didn't want to recall that moment too clearly. The
assistant had pulled back the shroud with the dismal satisfaction of a conjuror's assistant revealing that the trick
had failed to come off and Farmer and Alec had gazed
impassively down at what was left of Tracy Ashford. There
hadn't been much glamour in seeing her there. About as
much as she herself must have found in the tawdry studios
and dingy offices which were the reality of 'glamour modelling'.

'Definitely drowned?' Alec had asked.

'Nothing definite yet,' Farmer had replied. 'The PM'll be
done this morning. But our own chap's pretty sure she was
drowned. There are bruises too, as you see.' He nodded to
the attendant and they turned away. 'Poor bitch,' he said
heavily.

As they drove back to the police station Farmer had said,

'This isn't a large town, Alec, once you take away the tourists and the seasonal traders. It's rather behind the times, too, in some ways—deliberately so. You can guess how the youngsters feel. They see everybody just sitting about waiting to die, and they want to live. Local beauty queens like Tracy all get so-called "modelling" offers. I expect she weighed it up and decided it was her way out.'

'But the town council didn't like it?'

'Not much. What I could never work out was why they took so long to come to the point they did. The newspaper photo which cooked her goose didn't appear till a couple of months back, but she'd done a full spread in a girlie magazine as long ago as last New Year. Why didn't they jump on her then?'

'Maybe they never knew about it.'

'I find that hard to believe. Mind you, the newspaper photo actually mentioned the town and her title. Perhaps that was what decided them. I still don't know whether what they did was right. They were thinking of the families, of course, booking their holidays.'

'Who do you think buys the papers?' Alec had asked drily.

'The dads of those families, I know. But the mums book the holidays, don't they? Anyway, they decided it would be right for their image to drop her. Not that it was strictly their title to take away, but that wouldn't have worried them. They'd fix it easily enough.'

'Did Tracy come in for hate mail at all?'

'If she did, she made no complaints to us. The taking away of the title, though, did cause quite a stir locally. Letters in the paper, and so forth. The balance of opinion seemed to be that the councillors were behaving like old women, but some of the comments did get very personal.'

'You said there was another reason?'

'What?'

'Why you decided against suicide. You said she was naked when she was pulled out of the sea.'

'Mm. Actually, we do have a naturist beach here, though you won't find it mentioned in the brochures. It's in the next bay. Called the Haven. But even these days it's not easy to make your way to the beach of an English seaside resort stark naked, however few clothes you wear once you're there. So what happened to her clothing?'

'Um. How was the tide? About half way up, wasn't it?'

'That's right. Of course we don't know yet what time she went into the water. The tide was rising—high tide about six-thirty. So it's possible, if she undressed right by the water's edge, that her things were washed away almost at once.'

'Would you expect them to turn up again?'

'That's a tricky one. Once they were well waterlogged, maybe not. But we were pretty quick off the mark looking for them.'

'And you say a holidaymaker found her.'

'A holidaymaker spotted her,' Farmer corrected. 'A woman called Mrs Burch, out swimming not too far from the shore, saw her floating face down. Of course, she didn't go and see if she could help. People never do. Instead, she made her way back to the beach and spent ten minutes looking for a lifeguard. He swam out and brought her in, but he says he knew at once she'd had it.'

'Artificial respiration?'

'The lifeguard started it. My chaps carried on till the ambulance came. They say you can recover after half an hour under water, and one of the chaps says he thought at one stage she did show some sign of life, but his mate isn't so sure. Anyway, the hospital marked her dead on arrival.'

'What now, sir?' Pringle was standing blank-faced by the side of the smiling Tracy and Alec dragged his thoughts back to the present with an effort.

'Fix up an orders group.' He glanced at his watch. 'Make it for midday. When you've done that, make a start on sources of information. We want to build up a picture of her life, from age eleven or so. School, friends, holiday jobs, youth groups, relatives she loved or hated. Where she was living, who with. What she did when she wasn't at work.'

'Wouldn't it be better if I—' Pringle began.

'No, I don't think it would,' Alec said without emphasis, and met the sergeant's eyes impassively. He knew Pringle resented his presence; knew, too, that they had to work together despite it. It would be as well to get the message across at the start. Pringle paused, and thought better of whatever he had been about to say.

'Yes . . . sir. I'll get started.'

The phone went as Pringle turned away and Alec made himself pick it up slowly.

'Stainton.' The Superintendent, Alec's superior at County HQ, was characteristically curt. No so long ago he had been actively hostile, but now Alec realized they each had a respect for the other, even if they might be reluctant to admit it. 'Think it's murder? Or is this chap Farmer just raising the wind? Seaside policemen,' added the Super dismissively.

'It's suspicious, sir,' Alec said. He waited for the door to shut behind Pringle. 'I don't think he's the sort to start hares unnecessarily.'

'Right. I'm spoiling your holiday, Alec. Can't be helped. I'm not going to treat you like an idiot. You know what I want. Daily report. Speak to me before taking any drastic step. Now, who do you want? You probably can't have them. We're down to the bottom of the barrel as it is.' Thank you, Alec thought silently, for that encouraging remark. 'You can have Johnson again if you want. Is there anyone down there who's any use? What about that sergeant?'

'I think he'll be OK, sir. He's a bit prickly at the moment because I've invaded his patch.'

'More fool him. Sit on him firmly, if you have to. Just

Johnson, then?' the Super went on before Alec could inter-
vene. 'Good. Got a woman down there?'

'Well, I . . .'

'WPC,' the Super clarified shortly. 'Is there one at the
station or is she on leave or pregnant or something?' The
Superintendent was not a great believer in women having
careers in the police force.

'She's here, sir.'

'Right. You'll need her for all the weeping relatives.
Wasn't the dead girl involved in blue movies? Send her
along there. Open her eyes.'

'I don't think it's exactly blue movies, sir. Just the standard page three stuff.'

'Don't you believe it.' The Superintendent's snort carried
clearly down the line. 'Anyway, if you've a WPC you won't
be badgering me to send you your last chit. Simmonds.
Good. Get to work, then. No time to waste. Anything you
want, you ring me direct. Got it?'

The phone went dead and Alec smiled wryly at the
Superintendent's aggression. That same manner had put
backbone into more than one wavering subordinate before
now, and Alec suspected that there was little of it that was
not put on. The Super had been enjoying himself, too, Alec
was sure, teasing him about Jayne Simmonds. Well, he
could take that.

He thought bleakly of their happy cooperation on the
Swainson case, the only happy thing about it, and of the
promise that had seemed to be held out for the future, then
he pushed the thought stubbornly away and, running his
fingers through his hair, began to write.

On the sands, Cathy had had a miserable morning. Heather
had become increasingly uncommunicative as the hours had
passed and Alec had still not appeared. Perhaps, Cathy
thought, it had been a mistake to introduce themselves to
him yesterday, after all.

The two girls had swum, and oiled themselves, and read, and licked ice-creams, but there was no doubt it had been a dull day so far. Finally they had been accosted by a pushy youth who suggested they should all go for a swim together. Cathy had told him where to get off, and she felt sorry now as she remembered his hurt expression, like a puppy that has been kicked.

Cathy decided it would be better if they packed up and spent the afternoon in the amusement arcades, or took a bus ride into the country inland. The truth was, she thought bleakly, that their new friend had found them dull. It was clear, from the way he spoke, that he was used to clever people. Well, that couldn't be helped. She knew that she and Heather were ordinary. Only their youth and health, she admitted with painful insight, made them interesting. Yet . . . perhaps it was for the best. He was probably only after the usual thing. So why hadn't he persevered? She sighed, and glanced at her friend anxiously. Tonight she'd make sure they went out and enjoyed themselves. She wasn't going to have them sit moping in the apartment. Resolutely, she set herself to the task of cheering up Heather.

'Disgustin',' the Captain pronounced, glaring round the dining-room.

'What I don't see,' Miss Wynne-Andrews said in a reasonable voice, 'is why they took him away? What had he done?'

'What had he done? My dear lady. Body fished out of the sea in the afternoon. Chap hauled out of the hotel in the evenin' and off to jug. What does it look as if he'd done?'

'We don't know,' Miss Hanson said mildly. 'There may be no connection. He may have had bad news about a sick relative, mayn't he?'

'Pah,' the Captain retorted with more force than politeness. 'You don't come to tell a chap bad news with a police car skidding to a stop with all its lights on. You're too charitable, ma'am.'

'Well, I don't know,' said Miss Hanson wistfully. 'He seemed such a nice young man.'

'So was Crippen at that age, I expect.'

'I'm sure if a spell in the army was still compulsory,' Miss Wynne-Andrews said maliciously, 'we would see far less of this sort of thing.'

The Captain glared at her suspiciously. 'I don't know what it is,' she continued sweetly, 'that puts thoughts of killing people into their heads.'

'Damned unpleasant,' the Captain snorted, unsure whether he was being made fun of. 'Damn pretty girl, though. So they say,' he added.

Alec sat behind his desk and marshalled his thoughts. Beside him, Inspector Farmer watched him pensively, while Pringle, WPC Pink and the newly arrived DC Johnson were ranged against the farther wall on chairs from the canteen, waiting for whatever wisdom their seniors might manage to summon up. Johnson, in fashionable jeans and a loose sweatshirt, looked most at home. Used as he was to working with Alec, and disinclined to be impressed by Inspector Farmer, he was able to contemplate with satisfaction the benefit to his career of this new posting.

Detective-Sergeant Pringle waited composedly enough, concealing with the ease of practice his scepticism of the abilities of this young detective-inspector. He had, Pringle had heard, something of a reputation for maverick cleverness. That was not a recommendation.

WPC Pink (pink by name, and pink by nature, they had said when she joined the Force, but it took a lot to make her blush these days) waited patiently too. Whatever plan the two inspectors dreamt up, she knew her role would be the same. Interview the relatives, calm the weepers, handle the children. The women's jobs. That was the way of police forces no less than of the world, and she had ceased to try and make an issue of it when these tasks were handed out to her as a matter of course. She saw Alec's glance pass over her and contrived to look alert. She could not, however, look sexless, and grimaced as his gaze wandered from her face to her well-filled uniform shirt, and thence to the kneeling Tracy who peeked out over her shoulder. The last thing Liz Pink wanted was attention of the wrong sort from this aquiline DI.

'I want to build up a picture of Tracy Ashford,' Alec began at last, 'and you're the people who can help me do so. I'm a stranger to this town—so is DC Johnson. That cuts both ways. It means we have to start from scratch, but it also means that we're not known. The rest of you are. That's something worth bearing in mind. OK—' he hunted for the name; Pringle always seemed merely Pringle in his mind—'John. Would you kick off, please, with what you've found out so far, and then we'll set about filling in the gaps.'

Pringle pulled a regulation notebook from the pocket of his shirt and turned the pages. 'Tracy Louise Ashford. Born 5th February 1969. That makes her nineteen.' He paused and flushed, realizing that he had stated the obvious, then recovered himself. 'She's always lived in the town. Went to school at St James's—that's the C of E primary near her home—then the Captain Hardy Comprehensive. Left at seventeen, sir. She stayed on with the idea of doing A-levels, then apparently got bored when she saw her friends with money to spend—at least, that's the inference. She wasn't dim. Six O-levels and two CSE's. Good at games. Prefect in her last term.'

'When they already knew she was leaving, presumably,' Alec surmised. 'Possibly they didn't feel her to be up to it before?'

Pringle nodded, acknowledging the interruption. 'Up to a year ago, she was living with her parents. He's some sort of scientist and teaches at the hospital. Wife doesn't go out to work. There's a son, twenty-two, manager with the supermarket. Tracy kicked around for a month or two after leaving school, then landed a job as receptionist in a doctors' surgery. Her father's contacts may have got her that. After a year there, she got fidgety at home and moved out to share a house with some students from the Tech. Four of them, including her, two girls, two blokes. That was May last year, when she was eighteen, and at the same time she went in for the Southern Belle title. That was decided in August —holiday season, of course. That's all I've come up with so far, sir.' He looked from Alec to Farmer, but if he was anxious he didn't show it. 'I haven't talked to anyone about what sort of girl she was, or about more than the bare facts.'

'Regular boyfriend, do we know?' Alec asked.

Inspector Farmer cleared his throat. 'She was kicking about with a boy called Willie Henderson for a good while. He's a local lad. Last summer she had a fling with one of the trainees at the surgery. She's been known to see a fair amount of one of the showmen who runs one of the amusement arcades, but that may have come to an end last year.'

Alec looked at him curiously, and he shrugged apologetically. 'Daughters,' he explained. 'I asked them what they knew. They were all at school together. But they haven't seen much of her since she left her parents'.'

'I take it she'd have lost the Southern Belle title anyway in August?' Alec asked of the room at large. Pringle and Farmer nodded. 'So she wouldn't have worried too much at having it taken away a month early. She sounds something of a cool customer.'

'If she wasn't before, she is now,' said Farmer, grimly.

'Just so.' There was a little silence while they contemplated the inspector's remark.

Alec turned to Liz Pink. 'How far have you got with tracing her movements?'

'Not very far, sir. She was in work at the surgery the morning she died. They see patients from nine to eleven, then Tracy usually helps with the paperwork and the dispensary for an hour. She goes for lunch at twelve-thirty and that's the last time we know that anybody saw her.'

'What about the night before?'

'Don't know, sir. I didn't approach the housemates—Detective-Sergeant Pringle suggested I wait till we knew what sort of approach you wanted. She hadn't been home, I mean to her parents'.'

'Would you expect her to?'

'I don't think she made much of a habit of dropping in to see them, sir. I don't think they were very close.'

'Did you know her?' Alec asked curiously. Liz Pink raised her eyes to his briefly.

'You know most people in a place like this, sir. I did know her at school. She was lower down than me, of course, by several years.'

Alec stared abstractedly at the Tracy Ashford who smiled from the cheap newsprint pinned to the door. It was a mistake to assume there were no real communities any more. This town, at least, had been changed less than one might imagine by television and the motor-car. In a town like this envy, jealousy, indignation, would all ferment and corrupt insidiously and remorselessly.

He drew his mind back to the immediate problem. 'Inspector Farmer?'

'We've been looking for the clothes, of course,' Farmer said. 'Along the tideline. We also questioned the boatmen. Oh yes,' he answered Alec's look of surprise, 'there are still a few families here who live by what they catch. That doesn't just mean trippers. Several still set their lines and pots.'

'Anything?'

'Nothing. Not a sausage. We checked right round into the Haven, and even had one of our chaps rowed out to search the rocks off the point. Nothing.'

'It doesn't prove anything,' Alec said calmly, 'but necessary work all the same. Thank you. That just leaves the results of the PM.' He lifted a sheet of paper from the desk and let it drop again. 'According to this, Tracy died of drowning in sea water. The body shows signs of a struggle before death, but not severe enough to cause death in itself. The time of death seems to be anywhere between twelve and two-thirty. She was young, and fit, and that together with the fact that the body was in the water for a couple of hours means that the usual signs as to the time of death have to be interpreted with a little caution. It seems that there were marks received after death, as if the body had rubbed against rocks, or perhaps the legs of the pier, but the pathologist won't rule out the possibility of these marks too being deliberate. It looks as if an assailant hit her to subdue her before drowning her, and maybe went on hitting her afterwards. It's likely that she was pressed beneath the water by a hand clamped round the back of her neck, that is, by someone standing behind her.' He stretched his own arm out, the fingers in an open grip, and pushed his imagined victim remorselessly down on to the desk top.

'We don't know whether she was stripped before or after she was drowned,' he went on. 'There are no signs of sexual interference. Tracy seems to have had a normally active sexual life. She was on the pill. The marks of a struggle, of course, mean that the possibility of suicide can be virtually ruled out. I must say, from what I've heard, it didn't sound much in character anyway.' His eyes strayed back to the smiling pin-up. 'I can't see her swept away on a tide of remorse, can you?'

'No, sir,' Pringle said, but the remark didn't need an answer.

'So we assume it's murder. As Inspector Farmer wisely deduced from the outset.'

Farmer ignored the politeness. 'Are you going to be reinforced?' he asked tonelessly.

Alec looked at him quizzically, then let his gaze slide round the room from face to face. 'This is it,' he said evenly. 'Let's get on with it, then. John, I'd like these boyfriends chased up, please. Present whereabouts, and where they were on Tuesday this week. I'll want to see them each myself in due course. Will you see to that? Liz, we've lots more work to do on Tracy's movements before her death. It looks as if she certainly died in her lunch-hour. How did she normally spend it? Did she go home? Down to the beach? Find out. As soon as we have a photo, hawk it round the stores in town, and among the holidaymakers on the sands.'

'It might be as well to start with the sands this afternoon,' Inspector Farmer put in.

Alec nodded. 'Holidaymakers are creatures of habit. Those who were down there yesterday will likely be in the same place today.' Briefly, Alec's thoughts winged to Heather and Cathy. They too would be there again. He could be with them, if Tracy Ashford were still alive. 'Better check in—what do you call it?—the Haven, too,' he added.

'It's rather a lot of ground to cover, sir.'

Alec considered, then nodded. 'OK, Andy can take the Haven. You can also sort out the people she shared a house with. Get as much information as you can about the sort of life she was living this last year, when they last saw her, her state of mind, everything. I'd better make Tracy's parents my first port of call. OK, if anything turns up—let's have it directly. Let's move.'

CHAPTER 3

Alec's own inquiries were singularly unfruitful. Talking to Mrs Ashford, he very soon realized that she and her husband had cut their daughter off as ruthlessly as ever Victorian paterfamilias cast out his erring offspring. It was apparent, too, that where Tracy's 'modelling' was concerned Mrs Ashford had donned a complete and seamless veil of ignorance. Every time he approached the topic she sheered away without so much as acknowledging its existence. So far as her mother was concerned, Tracy had had a job as receptionist at the doctors' surgery and that was all. Why had the rift been made, and by whom? Alex, exasperated, decided there was little to be lost by asking outright.

'Rift?' Mrs Ashford echoed bleakly. 'Who's talking of a rift? She has her own life. If she's chosen to live it away from those who brought her up, that's her affair. She knows what's right, and she knows what's wrong. We taught her that, I do know.'

'But she doesn't call and see you, after work, in the lunch-hour maybe? It's not as if you live in different towns.'

'She lives her life and we live ours, that's all it is.'

'When she won the Southern Belle title, Mrs Ashford,' Alec said, trying a different tack, 'you were pleased for her, I expect.'

'I know nothing about that. I know we taught her right from wrong. Why couldn't she be like Terry?' It was a plea, and it escaped Mrs Ashford against her will, for on the instant she buttoned her mouth tighter still. The sitting-room they sat in was immaculate, every ledge crammed with knick-knacks, every chair precisely set, every cord and wire strictly regimented. Alec, looking about him, thought it verged on the obsessional, and found it easy to imagine the suffocation a normal, lively school-leaver would feel, pent in such a spotless prison.

'It's a bit late for wishing she was different,' he said heavily. 'She's dead. I have to find out how she died, Mrs Ashford, and why. Somebody killed her. Who?'

'Her father got her the job. A good job. Why couldn't she be content with it?' Something in the woman's inexorable plaint told plainly that Tracy's death was, for this parent, or a piece with her selfish young life.

'Who killed her?' Alec asked again. 'A boyfriend?'

'Don't ask me about boyfriends. She had enough boyfriends when she lived at home. She didn't have to go away for that.'

But Mrs Ashford, when questioned, could not or would not tell him any more. It was clear that she was simply unable to cope with her daughter's way of life, and Alec wondered whether, at bottom, it was disapproval or perhaps envy which had awoken such implacable hostility.

He left her soon after, hoping for better things from her husband. But Mr Ashford, when Alec saw him at the hospital, though more forthcoming, was hardly more enlightening.

'I wish we could have seen more of her,' he said apologetically. 'Kids these days ... I suppose they have to make their own way, but she didn't realize how her mother felt.'

Privately, Alec thought Tracy probably realized very clearly, and knew she must escape her mother's blackmail as soon as she could, or risk never doing so.

'And then,' Mr Ashford went on, 'what she's been doing since she won that title, it doesn't make my life here any easier, you know.'

'In what way, in particular?'

Mr Ashford looked embarrassed. 'This ... posing. You know. For the papers. It really doesn't make it very pleasant for me to know that all the staff have seen her, you know, like that. It's up in the porters' rest room, I know.'

'The newspaper pin-up?'

'Another one ... from a magazine. Not a very nice one,' he said in a small voice.

'Was it because of the posing that you and your wife decided to have nothing more to do with Tracy?'

Mr Ashford shrank from Alec's forthright question, as if he would have liked to deny it, but couldn't. Alec watched him speculatively, wondering whether he could really be as ineffectual as he seemed.

'How do you spend your time here, sir?' he asked curiously. The room they were talking in was fitted up as a small lecture theatre with a broad mahogany-topped bench for demonstration purposes.

'I do a mixture of teaching, for the nurses, you know, and lab work,' the other man replied. 'I've been here since Tracy was a toddler.'

'When I spoke to your wife, I asked her if she had any idea who might have killed Tracy,' Alec said. 'If I may say so, she accepted the idea of murder surprisingly readily. Do you find it easy to believe that someone could want to kill your daughter?'

Ashford's eyes shifted from side to side as if hunting for something he had mislaid. He said hesitantly, 'I don't know much about these things, Inspector. But . . . I can't imagine the circles she got into are very fussy about life and death, are they? Would someone, if she got on the wrong side of them, or wouldn't, you know, do the sort of things they want them to do . . . It's a hell of a way to have to talk about your own daughter,' he said sombrely, and Alec nodded, sobered by the other man's wan acceptance of the realities of his daughter's life.

'It's possible,' he said. 'It's just as possible that someone here felt themselves forgotten by her, or kept a grudge. Was outraged, or killed her in a fit of passion.'

'It seems unlikely. The boys she used to know all seemed such nice boys. Of course, they were only kids really, then. After she left home it was different, I suppose. I expect you realize that she and her mother were, well, rather cool. You see, we began to realize that the sort of life she was living was different from the one we might have liked for her. But you have to let them make their own mistakes, haven't you?'

'Perhaps you have. Perhaps your wife would have been wiser to follow your line on that. I suppose that's the worry of being a parent.'

'Yes.' Ashford nodded. 'When it happens to you, you'll realize. You care for them so much. Especially the girls. It makes it hard to accept that they must make their own way without you.'

Alec said, 'Was Tracy going to give up her job at the surgery? She must have earned a reasonable sum from the modelling.'

Ashford shrugged. 'I think they earn less than one imagines. Tracy is clever enough to value a good regular job, especially one which gave her so much freedom. If she was going to give it up, I hadn't heard, anyway.'

'When did you last see your daughter?'

Ashford shook his head sadly. 'Two months? Three? Oh dear, it must look so bad to you. We used to be such a close family, when the children were small.'

'But so far as you knew Tracy was cheerful, happy in her work, not anxious particularly?'

'I wonder whether we should have known, even if she had been anxious. If she'd been in some sort of trouble, I doubt if we'd have heard of it from her.'

There was little more to learn from Mr Ashford. As a matter of form Alec checked where he had been the day before, but he had been at work all day and his movements, it seemed, were easily verified. Alec was glad to leave him in the shabby, prosaic, echoing reception hall and walk out into the sunshine to thread his way tentatively through the back streets downhill towards the beach. Mats hung over balconies, buckets and spades sat in shady porches. A cat sauntered arrogantly along the very middle of a quiet street, tail erect, while others snoozed in basement areas or on the leaded parapets of the bay windows.

Down on the seafront, Alec looked this way and that for the white blouse of WPC Pink and spotted her a hundred yards away bending to speak to an elderly couple in deck-chairs. Their heads came together as they studied the photograph on her clipboard, then drew apart and Alec saw the shake of the head. He walked along to the next set of steps and intercepted Liz Pink in her progress along the sands.

'Any joy?'

Liz was flushed with the heat, and minute beads of sweat shone on her forehead. Her uniform skirt and shoes were not made for the beach, and her white blouse clung unbecomingly to the small of her back and across her breasts.

'Nothing, sir. Nobody seems to have seen her, but then, no one recognizes the girl in the photo as the Southern Belle girl, either.'

Alex said, 'Which picture are you showing them?'

Liz held out her clipboard. A demure young woman looked out from the photograph, head and shoulders, in soft focus.

'It was taken for her eighteenth, sir.'

'It's a bit different from the Tracy in the pin-ups,' Alec remarked.

'Yes, sir. That's what I thought. I have got a copy of the pin-up photo with me, actually, but I thought it might offend some of the older people, and distract them from actually trying to remember.'

'Care to let me have it?' Alec took the glossy and looked at it for a moment, then he neatly folded it horizontally a third of the way up from the bottom, tucking the bottom part back out of sight.

'Better?'

Liz saw a laughing, pert Tracy in necklace and earrings, with bare shoulders. Just the first swell of her bosom could be seen, and it was to the smiling, attractive face that the eyes were drawn.

'Lots better, sir.'

'Good. Look, don't forget to ask the vendors on the stalls up on the promenade, especially round the route she would have taken if she came down from the surgery. They spend their time watching for pretty girls.' He regarded her speculatively. 'Not finding it too much, in the heat?'

Liz Pink made a face. 'I'd do better in something cooler

than this, but I'll cope. I shan't pass out or anything, but I'll be dying for a swim before I'm done.'

'Too bad,' Alec said briefly. 'Inspector Farmer wouldn't look kindly on one of his officers stripping out of her uniform, Haven or no Haven.'

'Thank you, sir. I'll be all right,' Liz replied neutrally. 'The Haven isn't really my cup of tea.'

Alec nodded towards a family group along the beach. Lying on her stomach, propped on her elbows reading a book, the young mother was letting her naked back and tiny breasts tan, and neither she, nor her husband, nor her children either seemed at all embarrassed.

'A very moral little town,' Alec echoed to himself. 'Times are changing.' And Liz, glancing at the girl and back at Alec, thought he said it rather sadly.

Alec headed for the promenade and walked swiftly away from the pier towards the Logan Hotel. The crowds dawdled, and stopped in their tracks, and changed course without reason, and he wended his way with some difficulty. Instead of turning up towards the hotel, however, he turned smartly right and dropped down the stairs to the beach again.

He saw Cathy and Heather before they saw him, and his step unconsciously slowed as he watched them a moment unobserved. Cathy knelt on her towel, energy in every gesture as she urged some suggestion. Heather sat cross-legged. She was facing Alec, but her head was bent and she played with something on the sand, pushing it about with her forefinger, her dark hair swinging forward over her cheek. Sudden, total lust rose unbidden in Alec so that the saliva dried in his mouth and his limbs were suffused with luxurious urgency.

As he hesitated, Heather looked up and her scrabbling in the sand ceased, then Cathy too looked round, and he came up to them and his disconcerting desire was . . . not forgotten, but put to one side.

'We were trying to decide where to go tomorrow,' Cathy said. 'I want to go on the downs. We've been down here every day so far. We ought to do something else. You'd like it if we did,' she said to her friend, turning to her again, 'you know you would.'

Heather said nothing, her eyes searching Alec's and then dropping, awkwardly, to the sandy landscape enclosed by her tanned thighs and calves. Cathy grimaced, and said again, 'You would, once we actually did it. Why don't we?'

Heather said, 'Perhaps Alec is going to join us on the beach. He may not want to spend his day tramping over the downs.' Still her head was bent, her face hidden.

'I can't do either, I'm afraid,' Alec said. 'I came to tell you. I didn't want to just stay away and let you think I didn't appreciate your company. I haven't much time to myself, just at the moment.' And he gave them briefly the story he had decided on as he walked along the promenade, about his firm needing some extra work done which was keeping him busy all day.

'We understand,' Cathy said. 'It's rotten of them to spoil your holiday, all the same.' Doubt shadowed her face, nevertheless. If only his story weren't so pat—and so unlikely. No one knew better than she how dispensable the bigshots in the office actually were, once they were absent for some reason. Life went on as if they had never been there. Yet . . . she knew she wasn't very subtle, but she couldn't for the life of her see why Alec should bother with a fiction of that sort, unless possibly he was bored with their company but still cherished a hope of finding his way into their beds. Maybe he wanted to keep them in hand in case nothing better turned up? All of a sudden she wasn't sure she liked this elusive young man.

Alec, sensitive to her scepticism and to his own lie, sought to salve the situation. 'If I can, though, may I call one evening? I don't know for sure how I'll be fixed.'

Cathy looked at her friend.

'If you like,' Heather said quietly. Alec tried to make out her expression, but her dark hair shadowed her face.

'You can try, if you like,' Cathy said, looking straight at him. 'And if we're there, we're there.'

'All right. I'd like to, if my business lets me,' Alec said. He left them then, conscious that he must return to the station, unsure whether he might not have been wiser simply to let the friendship drop. Their interest in him, that first day they had spoken on the beach, had been mildly flattering, but he recognized, with distaste, that he was making the two girls serve a purpose they knew nothing of, sating himself with their straightforward physical attractiveness and their innocent warmth as a way of overcoming his depression at his rejection by Jayne Simmonds. He was calculating, too, on the transience of their stay. They would never form a lasting friendship. That was the very reason he let himself be drawn into their lives. If the outcome was a holiday afffair with one or other of them, then so be it. They must have accepted that possibility when they first approached him. Nevertheless, it did cross his mind that he might not manage to remain quite so disengaged in fact as he anticipated in theory.

Two hours later Alec and Detective-Sergeant Pringle rang the bell of the doctors' surgery where Tracy had worked and submitted to the baleful stare of a severe middle-aged woman.

'Detective-Inspector Stainton,' Alec said, before she could tell them the surgery was closed. 'I spoke to a Dr Bridger on the telephone.'

'I'll go and see if Dr Bridger can see you,' the woman said sceptically. Alec took a step forward.

'Thank you. We'll wait in here, shall we?'

Cheerfully, he led the way into the waiting area and took up an old copy of *Punch*. 'If you would tell Dr Bridger we're here, and ask him if he could make it convenient to talk to us straight away.' Alec had no intention of spending the rest of the evening languishing in the empty surgery, and imparted a crispness to his words which he modified with a polite smile. The woman left, and silence descended.

Five minutes later Dr Bridger, young, broad-shouldered, wary, came through and Alec stood up and held out his hand. The two men were of an age, and eyed each other appraisingly. Alec reached for his warrant card.

'You'd better see this, Doctor, then you'll know I'm who I say I am. And you're one of the partners here?'

'Mm.' Dr Bridger studied the warrant card carefully, before looking up. 'There are four of us, but I'm the only one here at present. The senior partner is away for the week. I'm number three in the pecking order, so you might want to consider whether you'd rather wait and speak to one of the others.'

Alec shook his head. 'I'll talk to you, if you can spare the time. I can always have a chat with your senior partner later. Can we go through somewhere?'

'Of course. You didn't say on the telephone what this was about, Inspector,' Dr Bridger said as he led the way down a corridor past the blood transfusion posters and the admonitions Not to Call your Doctor to a Home Visit unless Absolutely Necessary. 'If it's to do with one of the patients, I may not be able to help you much. You understand.'

He held a door open. 'In here.'

Alec took the proffered chair, while Pringle settled on one against the far wall. 'Do you really think it's to do with a patient?' Alec asked.

Bridger picked a pen off the desk and began to toy with it, scrutinizing the drug name on the side and pulling the cap on and off. 'Tracy Ashford?' he asked.

'Yes.'

'She's been drowned. Accident?' Alec said nothing. 'Of

course. That's why you're here.' Bridger looked unhappy, and Alec noted it and speculated. Unhappy because he liked Tracy? Because he shrank from the idea of a suicide, or murder? Or because it was inconvenient to have the practice associated with a suspicious death?

The doctor sighed. 'Okay, tell me how I can help.'

'Well,' Alec said slowly, 'there's the facts, about her work here; and your own impressions. Both are valuable.'

'She worked well,' Dr Bridger said. 'She'd been here, it must be, just over two years. Miss Buxted, who let you in, really runs the administrative side of the practice for us, and Tracy's job is to act as receptionist, deal with patients as they come in. Then she'd generally help between surgeries as required. She was a very good receptionist. The patients liked her.'

'Quite.' Alec could well imagine that it was pleasanter to be greeted by Tracy Ashford's youthful charm than Miss Buxted's middle-aged tartness. 'She worked hard at her job?'

'Yes.' Dr Bridger hesitated, conscious that something more was required. 'She fought a bit with Sybil—Miss Buxted—of course, but every one else got on well with her.'

'She was easy to be with?'

'Very.'

'Brightened the day? Made you feel good?'

'Well . . . yes, I suppose she did. She was always in good spirits. Not moody at all. And she was a very attractive girl. Inspector. She won a beauty title—Miss Southern Belle. She was very good-looking.'

'Just so,' said Alec. Bridger, embarrassed at his own momentary enthusiasm, banged the pen down on the desk and began to fiddle with a scratch pad instead.

Alec said, 'Apart from Miss Buxted, did women find Tracy good company? Or only men?'

Bridger hesitated. 'I suppose so. Not so much, perhaps.'

'She flattered men? Played up to them? Made them feel good in her presence?'

'Nothing excessive,' Dr Bridger said more sensibly. 'That wouldn't do if you were to work together. But, yes, I think we all felt a little bit brighter, a little bit more virile, maybe, for being in her company. It's not an uncommon phenomenon.'

'I'm sure. We're all lucky if we can work with people who have that effect,' Alec said. Sudden bitterness gave an edge to his voice and for a moment his gaze wandered round the room, over the posters, the desk lamp, the scales, as if he were puzzled to recall what he was doing there. Dr Bridger watched him curiously. Then habitual self-command took over once more, and he spoke more grimly in consequence of his lapse.

'Dr Bridger, to be frank, did Tracy use her attractiveness as a weapon? Did she make sure her sex appeal was always to the fore?'

'No,' Bridger said soberly. 'She knew, I'm sure, that she could have made any of us behave unwisely if she had tried. Middle-aged men aren't as sensible as they pretend. She had more sense than to let that happen. When I say she was good at her job, I'm being no more than just. We shall be hard pushed to find anyone as good to take her place. That's why we were so flexible over her modelling. So far as we could, we made allowances when she wanted time off and for her part she never asked for anything she knew it would be difficult for us to grant. She certainly didn't sit there giving us the come-on.'

'You're telling me just the sort of thing I want to hear.'

'I'm glad,' Dr Bridger said dismally, 'because it's only just beginning to sink in that she's dead. You wouldn't be here unless it was either suicide or murder. I suppose you won't tell me which it is?'

'No, but I'll ask you which you think more likely.'

'Not suicide. Tracy wasn't one to give in, if something

was troubling her. She was a fighter. But murder's such a terrible thought. Maybe the more terrible when the victim is someone as lively and as attractive as Tracy.'

'She wasn't cut out to be a victim?'

'She was cut out to be fallen in love with. If that doesn't sound too saccharine.'

'Not at all. Your impressions are valuable to me, Doctor, because I never met Tracy.'

'And you never will.'

Alec said deliberately, 'You had a trainee of some sort here last year, I gather. Tracy may not have set her cap at the partners, but she did so with him. Is that right?'

Bridger nodded. 'That's right enough. The rest of us kept a low profile on that one, because they didn't let it impinge on their work and we thought, rightly or wrongly, that their lives outside the surgery were their own business.'

'Quite. Did you get the impression that the affection was more on one side than the other, at all?'

'It was about even, I should say. Guy, the trainee, was swept off his feet by Tracy, there's no doubt about that. But it was far from one-sided. I rather fancied, though, that the relationship was more deliberate on her part. Bear in mind that she had just left home, and that he was someone coming into her world from outside, who would in due course be moving on again.'

'You think she had decided that this was the time to broaden her horizons?'

'Something like that. It was her first love-affair, let's say, as opposed to the usual boy-girl thing.'

'This trainee would be older than her?'

'Oh, good Lord, yes. Trainee doesn't mean someone straight from school, Inspector. It means a qualified doctor who's well on the way to becoming a GP in his own right. Guy would have been twenty-seven or -eight.'

'Do you know how it ended?'

'Guy's time here came to an end, and I rather formed the

impression that they decided to bring things to a natural close then. Certainly, Tracy didn't seem too depressed at his going.'

'But you don't know whether he found it so easy to come to terms with.'

Dr Bridger looked at Alec shrewdly. 'I have no information one way or the other.'

'Of course. Now, it was after that that Tracy went in for this beauty title we keep hearing about?'

'During, rather than after. Guy left here in October last year. Tracy must have had the title for a couple of months then. As for the modelling, that didn't take off until a few months ago. I know she did one or two promotional things last year when she won the title, and I imagine one thing led to another. She began to think she might have the makings of a career in it. And I honestly believe she might, if she hadn't been such a damn fool about it.'

Alec raised his eyebrows at the other man's vehemence.

'Sorry,' Bridger said. 'What I mean is, she allowed herself to be sidelined into what they call glamour photography. It was poor career management, but I expect somebody persuaded her it would lead to what you and I would call proper modelling.'

'And doesn't it?'

'I should hardly have thought so.'

'You seem to have kept quite up to date on the progress of her new career.'

'Mm,' Bridger said meditatively. 'I think we all wanted her to do well, and we all rather regretted that she took the line she did. Morality apart, it seemed she was throwing away any long-term prospects. I mean, these glamour models are two a penny, aren't they? Silly girls who kid themselves there's something exotic about being photographed with no clothes on. I should have expected Tracy to do better than that.'

Alec said, 'Did she talk about her work much? Her modelling?'

'Not much. I don't know whether she enjoyed it. I suppose to you, never having met her, she must sound depressingly run of the mill.'

They sat in silence for a moment, both thinking of the dead girl. Alec pictured the girl in the pin-ups—it was no good thinking of the cold relic in the mortuary drawer— and knew she hadn't the potential to be a top model. She had healthy attractiveness, but no quirk of exoticism or enigma. She might, none the less, have been more than another pouting pin-up in the constables' locker room and the works canteens.

'I must get on, I'm afraid, Inspector,' Bridger said apologetically.

'Of course. Thank you for talking to me.'

'Come back if I can help further. I don't suppose I shall be able to, but one would like to have done all one could.'

'Of course. May I have a chat with your Miss Buxted on my way out?'

'Sure. Through the waiting area and on the right—it's marked "Practice Administrator" on the door.'

Their last sight of Dr Bridger was of his melancholy face as he reached for the telephone. There seemed little doubt that the surgery would be a duller place for Tracy's passing.

'No better than she should have been,' said Miss Buxted primly and Alec, in his delight at actually hearing the words uttered, fought down an inane grin. 'Always running after the doctors,' Sybil Buxted went on. 'Always giving them the wide-eyed innocent look and making sure they had a good sight of her bust.'

'But good at her work,' Alec murmured, 'or so I gather.'

'As girls go these days,' said Miss Buxted grudgingly, 'which isn't saying much. She could read and write if you didn't make it too difficult for her.'

'And the patients found her pleasant, I expect.'

'Little minx. It suited her down to the ground, of course, being the centre of attention behind the reception desk, handing out appointments like Lady Bountiful. If you ask me, it's the attention she got here which put it into her head to go in for the modelling. If you can call it modelling,' she added as an afterthought.

'What would you call it?' Alec asked.

Miss Buxted sniffed censoriously. The tiny room where they talked, squashed among the filing cabinets, reeked of disapproval.

'What I call it is neither here nor there. The fact is that she should have had the decency to give up her job here once she embarked on that sort of thing. I don't know how she had the nerve to sit behind that desk as if butter wouldn't melt in her mouth when all she'd got had been spread over the papers for everyone to see.'

'She didn't dress provocatively here?'

'She didn't *dress* provocatively,' Miss Buxted said with careful emphasis.

'Tell me,' Alec said, 'was there a receptionist here before Tracy came?'

'It was part of my duties,' Sybil Buxted said. 'It was a doctors' surgery in those days, and not a travelling circus with practice nurses and health visitors and I don't know what.'

'Quite. Tracy's routine, now. I'd be glad if you could give me some information on that. Her movements, particularly in the last few days, may be of special importance.'

Miss Buxted pursed her lips and bent her head in thought, but when she began to speak she was lucid and to the point and Alec understood why, though she might be abrasive, she would none the less be an asset to the practice.

Tracy had worked a nine to six-thirty day, but with a two-hour break at lunch-time. Miss Buxted, when pressed, agreed that Tracy rarely seemed to go home for lunch,

although there would have been ample time to do so, prefer-
ring to spend her time around the shops or on the beach.
Sometimes she would swim, coming back with her hair still
damp. Over the last six months the partners had increasingly allowed her to take her annual leave in day or half-day
packets, or even to have the odd afternoon off altogether,
an indulgence, needless to say, which Miss Buxted viewed
as calculated to encourage the worst traits of self-importance
and vanity in the girl.

These were for modelling assignments, she confirmed,
and the latest had been the previous week.

Alec turned to the last few days and found, as he expected,
that there was little to mark them out from any others as
far as Tracy's behaviour at work was concerned. Interestingly, she had returned from her modelling assignment in
low spirits, but had soon recovered her normal good humour,
and her normal inclination, Miss Buxted said disapprov-
ingly, to be cheeky if rebuked.

'What sort of things did you have to pull her up on?' Alec
asked.

'Well, you know,' said Miss Buxted, showing the first
signs of being uncomfortable under Alec's questioning, 'it
was more her general attitude. Her outlook, if you know
what I mean.'

It was more a question, Alec thought privately, of you
and she being totally antipathetic to each other. If she was
as prickly with you as you clearly were with her, it's a
wonder you managed to work in the same building at all.

Aloud, he said, 'Did you have to tick her off about
anything in particular this last few days? You said she was
cheeky again, when rebuked.'

'I passed a comment, which she chose to take as criticism.
On the way she was dressed. It was unnecessarily skimpy.'

'But you said she normally dressed well enough at work.'

'So she did. But not yesterday.'

'Yesterday? The day she died? How was she dressed?'

'Inadequately for a doctors' surgery. A linen skirt, and some sort of sun top. It was the top that was inadequate.'

'And you said as much to her. What was her reaction? Can you remember her exact words?'

Miss Buxted, a conscientious if reluctant witness, searched her memory. 'She said, as far as I recall, something like, "It's good enough for what I want it for, and if it's not good enough for you, that's just too bad."'

'"It's good enough for what I want it for"?'

'Or words to that effect.'

'Did you draw any sort of meaning from that remark?'

Sybil Buxted paused thoughtfully. Once her mind was applied to a problem she was at once less acerbic and far more likeable. At length she said, 'I think, if I drew any conclusion, it was that she had dressed for one particular person, or possibly for a particular situation, an interview, say. But more likely a person.'

'To attract that person?'

'Or to taunt them. I don't know why I say that. It must have been something in the way she spoke. You know,' she went on, 'I rather wish I had known her better, and could feel that we got on. I should have tried to show her that I did appreciate the way she worked: she really was quite efficient. She thought me a dreadful old maid. Perhaps that led me to behave like one. I wasn't really very nice to her, Inspector. I wonder now if it wasn't just envy on my part.'

'Of her youth, or her beauty?'

'Or even of her naughtiness. We envy others when they go that little bit further than we have ever allowed ourselves to go, don't we?'

'I expect you're right. But reproaching yourself won't help her now.'

'I just wish I'd realized it at the time. It's too late to have regrets now she's dead, isn't it?'

'Yes,' Alec agreed. 'It's too late.'

CHAPTER 4

Nine-thirty the next morning found Alec waiting with WPC Pink in the headmaster's office at the Captain Hardy Comprehensive School while the headmaster himself finished morning assembly. The paperwork and the planning had dragged on well into the previous evening, but Alec knew that the inquiry was well in hand. This morning he had held a second short briefing session and he waited now with reasonable patience for the headmaster's appearance. His only regret was that he had had no time the previous evening to call on Cathy and Heather. Perhaps there would be an hour to spare tonight. Liz Pink looked about her curiously, and Alec smiled.

'Does it awaken fond memories?'

She glanced at him. 'I was just thinking how ordinary it looks. Just like one of our offices at the station. Yet when I was a kid this place was terrifying.'

'Perhaps it was the occasions which terrified. Was this where you came to be ticked off?'

She grinned. 'Only if you were really wicked. I only came here twice. Once to be told I was being made a prefect. Once, before that, when I was fetched out of lessons to be told my father had died. I was thirteen. My first thought was how shabby my mother looked sitting here in such a grand place.'

'Children are terrible,' Alec agreed.

'Tracy might have come here more often. I do remember that none of the prefects could cope with her, and not many of the teachers either. That's why she'd have ended up here.'

'Was she so naughty?'

Liz shrugged. 'There were worse. But she was harder to handle than most. She didn't see why she should do what you wanted without a good reason. And as most of us were still at the "because I tell you" stage, she would just laugh and go her own way.'

The headmaster's account when, flustered and apologetic, he appeared, was in similar vein. Tracy had been something of a challenge to authority. On the whole, it was ordinary naughtiness, but there had been occasions, such as one unpleasant episode when a science master, overburdened with personal problems, had been reduced to tears by the concerted efforts of a group of which Tracy was the ring-leader, which left a nastier taste in the mouth.

'Academically bright?' Alec asked.

'Oh yes. A good mix of CSEs and O-levels. She would have done moderately well at A-level, but I think she was clever enough to realize that at university, say, she would be at the lower end of the spectrum. So she opted for what turned out to be a very worthwhile job at the health centre.'

'When the bother blew up about her appearing in pin-ups,' Alec asked, 'did you have any thoughts yourself?'

'About her, or about the town council?' The headmaster grimaced. 'The councillors made prize asses of themselves, in my opinion. But as for Tracy, I suppose I was rather disappointed. I should have expected her to see the limitations of what she was getting into. I couldn't decide whether she was deceiving herself, or deliberately trading on the seedier aspect so long as it lasted. Either possibility was unpleasant to accept because I had previously had rather a good opinion of her common sense and, well, decency.'

'So there was nothing in her life here that foreshadowed the turn her career took? There do tend to be some girls in every school who are known for their relaxed moral outlook.'

'True. Though as often as not it is more reputation than fact. I can't always pick up the nuances of the children's reputations among themselves, but I shouldn't have said she had a name for being at all loose. She had a lot of the boys after her, of course, so she had to be accustomed to fending them off and making it seem like fun. I should have said her sense of her own privacy was moderately well developed.'

'No stripteases at the sixth-form dance?' said Alec. 'No accidental little glimpses of what shouldn't be glimpsed?'

'No. No more than the usual pieces of daring they all indulge in at that age. As I said, it seemed out of character for her to do the sort of photographs she did, and I had to assume it was done rather cynically, and for rather a lot of money.'

'Mm.' Alec was noncommittal. 'I don't think the money would have seemed all that generous, if she'd had real scruples to overcome. Now, as to people she was close to. Boyfriends in particular. Is there anyone who ought to be included in our list that you know of?'

'I doubt it. When you rang, I did a little checking of my own, among the staff and so forth, without making too much of it. Tracy's only serious attachment here seems to have been to a lad called Henderson, and I think on Tracy's part it was never going to be more than close friendship. She also seems to have gone about in the summer holidays with a boy from London. He was only down in the season, to run some sort of booth or amusement arcade for his parents. Consequently, he is a bit of an unknown quantity to us.'

'Tell me about Henderson.'

'Oh, a nice lad. Not as bright as Tracy, but a hard worker, if you gave him something to aim at. He's with an estate agent now, inland. He stopped to chat a month or so back, driving a very new car. That'd be the firm's of course, but he looked quite well-to-do.'

'And he was fond of Tracy?'

'Oh, very fond. No doubt about that. I shouldn't be at all surprised if he was still very much attached to her indeed. I don't imagine he liked the turn her career was taking.'

'Would he try to stop it in some way?'

The headmaster looked at Alec shrewdly, and chose his words with care. 'I don't think he would try to affect things in any practical way. He might try to use whatever influence he thought he had. But influence of that sort is a wasting asset. You only keep it by not trying to use it too much.'

'You always kill the thing you love,' Alec said tentatively.

The other man sighed. 'Maybe,' he said reluctantly. But something drove him to add, 'When Henderson was younger, he only twice got into real trouble here.'

Alec said, guessing, 'Temper?'

'Horrific. But, as I say, rarely seen, thank God. Perhaps he grew out of it. They often do.'

As they walked back to the car, Alec said to Liz, 'Did you know about Henderson's fierce temper?'

'I'd forgotten it, sir,' Liz said, and then added, honestly, 'I think.'

'There's no room for that sort of forgetting in this job,' Alec said bitterly. 'Not in a murder, not in any criminal investigation. If you can't approach the case dispassionately, you're no use to me.'

'This is my own town, sir.'

'Do you think I don't know that? You know all these people. You know their mums and dads, you know their brothers and sisters. But you can't, you really can't, stop doing your job for fear that one of them might get hurt. You can't.'

They reached the car and faced each other across the roof. Liz said, 'I found myself thinking last night, sir, that I know the person who killed Tracy. I don't mean I know who did it, but I know them. It's someone I was at school with, or someone I see in the supermarket, or drink with in the pub.'

'It's likely,' Alec said. 'It's not inevitable.'

In the end she said, her face averted, 'I'll cope, sir. I'll forget it. I'll do the job all right. I'm sorry I said what I did.'

As they drove away, Alec said, 'You needn't feel sorry at saying it. I'm glad you felt you could.' A fleeting smile rewarded him, and they drove back to the station with a tiny link of comradeship forged between them.

Back at the police station Alec began to sum up his notes for the growing file. The room was his now, the cleared desk evidence of his occupation as much as the open windows and the empty ashtrays. There was a knock at the door and Pringle entered, taking a seat at Alec's nod with a perceptible relaxation of tension.

'About those two boyfriends, sir,' he began. 'The young one, Henderson, is no problem. You'd like to see him?'

'We'll both go,' Alec said. 'Arrange it for today if you can. Ask his boss just to make sure the lad's available, without mentioning us to the boy yet. And the doctor?'

Pringle's brow furrowed. 'He's up in the Midlands, sir, but it's taking a long while to track him down. Everybody says they'll ring back, and the day's passing before you hear anything.'

'It's annoying. But we'll have to see him in the end. For the time being, we'll get him interviewed by his local force, once you've found out where he is. Anything more?'

'Liz went down to the beach again when you got back. She's just popped in and asked me to give you this. She's gone out again, and so's DC Johnson, sir. And the Superintendent's coming in an hour. I think he'd quite like you to be around, sir.'

'I'm sure he would,' Alec said drily. 'OK, I'll be here. Keep plugging away at these contacts. It's routine sort of work, but you know as well as I do how necessary it is.'

When Pringle had gone, Alec lifted the few papers out of the wire tray on the desk and began to leaf through them. Liz Pink's notes, hastily typed on a single sheet, were brief but rewarding. Tracy Ashford had been seen just before one on the day she died by a candyfloss salesman whose stall was set up midway between the pier and the road down from the town centre. The identification was pretty positive: the man had recognized her as Miss Southern Belle, whose career he had followed with some interest since the furore about her modelling first broke. She had passed within a yard or two of his stall, heading away from the town centre and walking as if she was going somewhere and not merely out for a stroll. He couldn't say where she had gone after she passed him, because trade was brisk with the good weather, so there was no knowing whether she had gone down on to the beach, on to the pier, or turned up a side road. Alec refreshed his memory of the town from a street map. From where she was seen, Tracy could even, if she continued along the esplanade past the pier, have come out on the undercliff walk that ran in front of Cathy and Heather's apartment, or crossed the headland to the Haven. If she had been going there, though, she would have saved time by heading directly westward from the surgery, rather than coming down to the seafront first.

So far, Liz had discovered no one else who had seen her, but she planned to return to the area beyond the pier this afternoon to try, if possible, to establish Tracy's path and thus her destination.

Johnson was still out, but the fruit of his morning's labours was in the tray: a list of the photographic agencies and studios Tracy was known to have worked for. In all, there were fifteen photo sessions listed, for seven different photographers. In the last few months, one, Glamourpix, had been visited four times. Some of the sessions bore cryptic footnotes. 'Ears only', said one, and another, 'Neck'. Alec contemplated the prospect of tramping the back studios of London without enthusiasm. Nevertheless, it was valuable work.

The phone shrilled, and as he glanced at his watch Alec knew what it would be before he lifted the receiver. The Superintendent's arrival had thrown the little station into fluster, as the desk sergeant's nervous voice witnessed. Two minutes later, an equally nervous uniformed constable knocked on the door and shrank back to let the Superintendent enter. Alec was interested to find that he regarded the Super with something like respect and he noted an answering flicker of, at least, tolerant amusement in the other man's bluff gaze.

''Morning, Stainton.'

''Morning, sir.'

The Superintendent settled his bulk ponderously in the chair opposite Alec and regarded him critically.

'I've got fifteen minutes, Alec. No more. Tell me how it's shaping.'

Alec gave the Superintendent the background of the case as economically as he could, and listed the inquiries he had put in hand so far. The Super listened impassively, and picked a glossy of Tracy Ashford from the tray.

'This the girl?' Alec nodded. 'Pretty girl,' the older man said gruffly. Alec remembered that he had a daughter of his own, and kept silent.

'And you're sure in your own mind it wasn't suicide?'

Alec outlined the post-mortem findings and the Super nodded grimly. 'I'll interview this doctor chap myself. You can come with me. Likewise this photographer she did so much work for. Glamourpix.'

'Of course, sir.'

'I fancy weight might help there. So far as the rest of the interviewing goes, I trust you to call me in whenever it's appropriate.'

'I'll do that, sir.' They walked together to the station entrance and stood side by side on the steps.

'Too bad about your holiday, Alec,' the Superintendent said, sniffing the air. The sunbaked, dusty square basked in the heat, and even the traffic growled half-heartedly, as if complaining of the exertion.

'I'll take some time later in the year, sir.'

'If you can. Too few men, Alec. Too few reliable ones, at any rate.'

And with that terse, unexpected approbation the Super descended the steps and made his way to his car.

It was well into the afternoon by the time Alec and Detective-Sergeant Pringle began to climb the valley road out of the town. Pringle drove, and Alec had time to look around at the dusty countryside and wonder that they could be engaged on something as brutal as a murder inquiry when all about them suggested only leisure and relaxation. Holidaymakers' cars pottered lazily along, and even the delivery vans seemed in no particular hurry. Alec wondered whether Cathy and Heather were walking the downs somewhere just out of his sight, and whether he would have the opportunity to enjoy the simple, uncomplicated holiday friendship they had offered.

Until a year ago, the office of Plush, Wilkinson and Partners had hunched unchanged by the narrow pavement of the market town for a century or more. Posters advertising farm auctions long forgotten had stood in the window, as if more forthright advertising were hardly in the best of taste, and succeeding generations of Wilkinsons had contentedly reaped the harvest their forebears and the vanished Plush had sown so long ago.

Twelve months had brought a startling change. Plush, Wilkinson and Partners was now PWP Properties, a branch of a multiple agency chain owned by a big insurance group whose marketing consultants had shrewdly kept the quaintest of the auction posters to adorn the manager's office, while in the plate glass window slowly revolving displays advertised tastefully renovated period houses, unique barn conversions and artisans' town cottages full of a wealth of period detail. Inside, trim girls in matching skirts, blouses and shoulder length fair hair sat behind matching leatherette desks in the open-plan office whose sixteenth-century origins had just managed to defeat the designers' passion for regularity and squareness.

The office manager, alert and businesslike in conservative pinstripe, hurried forward from a back area to take charge. Henderson, it appeared, was awaiting them in the manager's own office, which he would happily put at their disposal. Time was no problem—these days the office stayed open until seven—and he would have a cup of coffee brought up to them directly. Alec thanked him courteously and they followed him to the first-floor office where Willie Henderson waited nervously under the auction posters.

Alec settled himself behind the manager's desk and regarded the lad carefully while Pringle set himself a chair just out of the boy's line of vision and took out his notebook. Henderson, for all his neat suit and Paisley tie was, Alec judged, no more than twenty, tall and gangling but with intelligence as well as wariness in the look he returned to Alec. They waited while one of the girls brought in a tray with two cups of coffee, and a plate of biscuits. There was no coffee for Henderson, Alec noted. The manager was waiting to see which way the cat jumped. Finally the girl bustled out and Alec leant back and smiled encouragingly.

'Well, Willie, you've been here two years now, I gather. Like it?'

The boy nodded. 'It took a bit of getting used to at the start, what with always wearing a suit and that. But it's a good job. They pay you according to what you earn for them, see, and I like that. If you do well, you earn more, and they promote you according to what you can achieve and not how long you've been here.'

'What do most of your mates do, from school? Are they in similar jobs to this?'

'Not many. One's in a bank, that's pretty good, but mostly they work in the canning factory or in the hotels. I reckon I'm pretty lucky.'

'Tracy Ashford was pretty lucky, too, wasn't she? I'm

told she was very good at her work and they thought a lot of her at the surgery.'

'She would be good. She'd be good at whatever she did.' Willie Henderson was emphatic and Alec, watching him carefully, thought it was an honest assessment, not born merely of infatuation. As if guessing his thoughts, the boy went on, 'There was nothing special between me and Trace. We were good friends. Mates, like. But I wouldn't want you to talk to people about her and get the wrong impression. She was all right.'

'Do you think I might get the wrong impression?'

The boy nodded soberly. 'There are enough people ready to call her names. They'd blacken her as soon as look at you. Ones that used to be her friends, too. They're jealous, that's what it amounts to.'

'You thought a lot of her.'

'I did. She was OK, Trace.'

'And now she's dead, I'm sorry to say. You knew that, of course?'

'Yes.'

'People have suggested she killed herself. Does that make sense to you?'

Henderson shook his head. 'That's the first thing I thought of. I don't think she'd do that. Why should she?'

'You tell me.'

'It just doesn't seem likely.'

Alec said, 'What about all this trouble over her beauty title? Wouldn't that have made her depressed? And she didn't get on with her family, I gather. Maybe it all got too much for her.'

'You don't know Trace.' The boy pulled a face, wry and rather sad. 'She wasn't the sort to get sorrowful because other people didn't like her. She had her life all sorted out, and it was going her way.'

'When she began the modelling, were you pleased for her?'

'Sure.'

'And were you so pleased when she started doing photos for girlie mags?'

Henderson looked uncomfortable. 'I thought it was stupid. Where did she think it was going to get her? And it wasn't very nice, knowing blokes were leering at her. I couldn't see how she could let herself do it. She was really choosy about people. Didn't like the lads at school who were always talking dirty and bragging about what they'd been up to.'

'Yet,' Alec said gently, 'she'd been going out with one of the doctors from the surgery, hadn't she? She couldn't have been quite the same innocent girl she was at school, you know.'

'She wasn't innocent,' Henderson said. 'Who is? But that doesn't make her a slut.'

'Were you and she lovers?'

There was a long pause. The boy looked down at his hands, lacing and unlacing the fingers. At length he said, 'We were once. Three years ago. Trace was sixteen.' He looked up, a curious mixture of emotion displayed in his face. He sighed. 'If you want to know the truth, she made me do it because she wanted to know what it was like. So that . . .' he stopped miserably.

'So that when someone came along whom she really cared for, she wouldn't be inexperienced,' Alec finished for him.

'Yes.' The single word dropped heavily into the space between them. On the floor below, typewriters clacked busily, and the bright voices of the receptionists drifted up to them as they sat, Alec with his eyes fixed on the boy, Henderson staring miserably at the desk, yet still defying their pity. 'I didn't hold it against her,' Henderson added finally. 'I never could see quite straight where Trace was concerned. She must sound awful to you, but you didn't know her.'

'She does sound rather ready to use people to help her achieve her own ends. Yet from what I gather, you stayed quite good friends, even when she began to look elsewhere for her sexual needs.'

'I probably shouldn't have taken it so meekly,' the boy said with a grimace. 'Like I said, I never saw straight with Tracy.'

'So you stayed good friends right up to her death?'

Henderson hesitated. 'To be honest, we weren't on very good terms these last couple of weeks.'

'Why was that?'

'Maybe she got tired of her old friends, what with all the people she was meeting in London. We must have seemed pretty much like yokels to her.'

'There's something else, isn't there?' Alec said. 'What did you do? Or was it something you said?'

'I . . . I told her I thought what she was doing was a mistake. She didn't like me interfering, of course. I tried to put it in terms of her career—how it would only stop her ever becoming a top model—but I expect it just sounded as if I was parroting the usual small town morals.'

'So you had a row.'

'Yes.'

'What did you do? Go out and get drunk? Smash up a telephone kiosk? Go round and beat her up? You've a fearful temper when you're roused, haven't you, Mr Henderson?'

'I . . . I just accepted it.' It didn't sound very convincing. 'I suppose I felt it was bound to come sooner or later. She'd moved beyond us. Moved beyond me.'

'And who killed her?'

'Not me,' the boy said angrily. 'But if you find out, just keep them away from me, that's all I ask. You can lock them up and throw away the key so far as I'm concerned. And don't let anyone say to me that she deserved all she got, just don't let anyone start saying that, or you'll have another murder on your hands, I tell you straight.'

'People will say it, you know,' Alec said, watching the boy's strained, white face.

'Yeah,' Henderson sighed. 'They'll be saying it already, I know. But it isn't true. Nobody deserves to be murdered. Trace least of all.'

'You're telling me you loved her.'

'Yeah, I guess I am,' Henderson said sadly.

'He wasn't telling us the whole story,' Pringle said as they drove away.

'No, I don't think he was,' Alec agreed.

'He could have killed her. He was out showing buyers round houses that day. He had only to fix the appointments and a bit of fast driving would have got him to the coast in no time. Plenty of motive, with her throwing him over.'

'You're right, of course. It's a possibility. You'll have to check out each of those appointments and find out what time they actually took place.'

'Right,' said Pringle happily. Alec knew he was already drawing up a chart in his mind, with distances and times marked on it, to show how Henderson could have killed the girl he loved, and smiled wryly. If only things could be so simple.

Liz Pink had found no one else who recalled seeing Tracy Ashford on the seafront on the day of her death, and Johnson's afternoon at the Haven had been even less productive, the occupants of the beach shrinking away like a receding tide from his advance. Alec, writing out his report that evening in the quiet office, felt they had had about the usual mix of success and frustration which normally attended the early stages of an inquiry. He looked at his watch and signed his name at the foot of the page. There was no more that could usefully be done until the morning, and it was still not too late. Something had been nagging him and he wanted to sort it out.

The light had faded from the sky, but the evening was as gentle as the day had been and when he came to the seafront he turned, not east towards the hotel, but westward, following the path Tracy Ashford must have taken on that last day of her life. He passed the pier with its twinkling lights and throbbing music and, reaching the point where the path divided, took the upper way towards Cathy and Heather's apartment.

When Cathy had answered his ring, and they all three sat on the diminutive balcony, Alec unburdened his mind and told them simply who he was and the nature of the 'business' which his 'firm' had thought important enough to interrupt his holiday. He paid them the tribute of the truth, and acknowledged aloud his need for somewhere to come from time to time where he was not the superior officer, nor they the subordinates, and where for an hour or two he could unwind.

'I knew you were having us on,' Cathy said with satisfaction. 'They just don't call people back off holiday in any office I've worked in. You're not having us on now, though, are you?'

'Do you think I might be?'

'Men'll try anything if they think it'll impress you,' she said darkly.

'I'll show you my warrant card, if you like,' Alec smiled.

'Well, I don't know. Perhaps we'll decide to believe you. Isn't it exciting?'

Heather, who had been sitting with her face hidden in the shadow of her dark hair, spoke. 'If you want to come here in the evenings, like you have tonight, you must. We'll be here. But you'll be busy during the day, won't you? Don't worry about that. You don't owe us anything.'

They were easier with each other after that, and sat companionably in the warm evening air while Cathy recounted their day on the downs and Heather, from time to time, put in a word of correction or of confirmation.

It grew late, and Alec rose to leave. Cathy kissed him on the cheek. Heather touched him briefly on the hand. Come when you can, they said, and don't worry if you can't. We understand.

The lights along the promenade still glittered but there were few people about and the music which drifted from the pier was slower and more romantic. Couples dawdled head on shoulder back to their rooms, and spurts of laughter hung on the air.

Only the late night television seeping under the bedroom doors disturbed the silence of the Logan Hotel and Alec made his way to his room unseen by the Captain or Miss Wynne-Andrews, to drift contentedly into sleep to the distant wash of the surf on the empty beach.

CHAPTER 5

First thing the following morning, Alec held a brief conference in his office to review the situation. There were major gaps in Tracy's contacts to be followed up, and they still knew far too little of her movements the last morning of her life. He set John Pringle to follow up the trainee GP, Guy Ricchi, as a matter of urgency, and asked Johnson to concentrate on the showman, or stallholder, Tracy was known to have gone around with.

He turned to Liz Pink. 'I've got to ask you to keep slogging away at tracing her path after she left the surgery on Tuesday. I'd also like you to arrange for me to see these students she lived with this evening, and I'd like it if you'd come with me.'

'The Super's picking you up at two, sir, to go to the photographer's,' Pringle said.

'I know. And before that I want to see the leader of the tourism committee on the council, to find out how Tracy took being robbed of her beauty title. Andy, you'd better come with me on that.'

Alec was not surprised, when he rang Richardson Plastics, to be told that Mr Richardson was engaged and would ring him back. It was no more than five minutes later, however, that Richardson returned the call with a courteous invitation to join him for lunch. Alec declined the offer, and politely pressed for an earlier meeting. Could they come right away? Of course, if they wished, was the reply, but there was a perceptible lessening of warmth to it none the less.

Richardson Plastics occupied the largest of a dozen units on a trading estate on the inland edge of the town. At one end of the building was a three-storey office block, where Alec and Johnson found the receptionist expecting them.

'Mr Richardson will see you in the board room,' the girl said. 'I'll have someone show you the way.'

The room to which they were ushered, on the top floor of the block, was unexpectedly pleasant, and sufficient testimony to the success of Richardson's business—which was, thought Alec, perhaps why he had chosen to see them there. Picture windows looked out to the swell of the downs, while the walls were panelled in some light wood which caught the sun and reflected it warmly. An expensive modern table stood against one wall, while from a group of chairs by the window Richardson himself rose to greet them. Short, and with a tendency to stoutness, in a conventional suit and with thinning hair, he was the typical local businessman and councillor. The eyes that met Alec's, however, were shrewd, although they seemed good-humoured enough.

'I'm glad you could come,' he said when the introductions had been made. 'A sad business. I was debating with myself whether to get in contact with you. It's worrying to think that her death might have any connection with the council's decision to remove her title.'

'Do you think it has?'

'It's been a worry to me. To think that she might have been depressed, or brought unduly low by it. You'll have some coffee? And I'll order some sandwiches while we talk.'

He spoke into a house phone set into the panelling, and gestured them to a chair. 'How shall we start?' he said. 'How can I help?'

'I'd like to understand the background to this matter of the Southern Belle title,' Alec said. 'In case, as you say, it has any bearing at all on what happened.'

'Of course.' Economically, Richardson began by outlining the political microcosm of the town, and the functions and responsibilities of the Leisure and Tourism Committee, of which he was chairman. 'The town's changing, of course. That's inescapable. Already there's precious little left of the seaside town that people came to in the 'fifties and 'sixties. We've broadened the base of the town's economy, with a certain amount of light industry and a growth in service jobs. In a minor way, we've become something of an out-of-town office location, though there's a natural limitation placed on that by our geographical position. We just haven't the communications of somewhere like Brighton. That suits us. But the real change is one you'll recognize all over the country. Attitudes have changed. People want a more sophisticated type of holiday now. If you came here for your week's holiday in nineteen-sixty or even nineteen-seventy, you ate in your boarding-house. Of course you did. Where else could you eat, unless you wanted a daily diet of fish and chips and whelks?

'Now, people come here to self-catering apartments. They may eat in, but if they eat out they want to eat well, and they know if they're not doing so. If they sunbathe, they see no point in doing so in shirtsleeves, braces and a knotted handkerchief. They come here as a change from Spain or France, and they bring here the standards and the expectations they've learnt in those places.

'Our problem is twofold, I think,' he said, eyeing them

carefully to assess how closely they followed him. 'One aspect is that we are still in transition. We still do have a sizeable holiday population made up of just those people you might have seen on our beaches twenty years ago. People who don't want to move with the times. Who want continuity. So the other part of the equation is our need to cater for these people. There aren't very many places now where they can find what they found all those years ago. They don't want the wine bars, they want the sand, and the dusty exhibits in the museum if it's wet, and the bus rides up on to the downs for a cream tea.'

'And you've chosen to meet their needs.'

Richardson nodded. 'We've chosen to keep the rate of change slow. We like these people. They don't spend so much money, perhaps, but nor do they cost us much to keep them happy.'

A white-coated waiter wheeled in a trolley with coffee in a silver pot, cups and saucers, and plates of sandwiches. Alec eyed the display sceptically.

'I wanted to say all that,' Richardson said, offering the plates to Alec and waving the waiter away, 'so that you get some perspective on the way our minds worked in the committee when we considered the problem Tracy Ashford had set us.' He frowned, and sighed. 'People will think us vindictive, Inspector. Nothing could be further from the truth.'

'I do find myself puzzled, though,' Alec said. 'Why didn't you just let Tracy's time as Miss Southern Belle expire of its own accord? Surely there was only a month or so left? Did you want to make a fuss?'

'I suppose in a way we did,' Richardson said meditatively, and bit purposefully into a sandwich. 'We wanted to get the message across that we were a little reactionary. A little behind the times. Perhaps more so than we actually are.'

'And the value of Tracy's title as advertising was coming

to an end. It was a useful way of squeezing a little more mileage out of it for the town.'

Richardson's smile became a little wary. 'You make us sound very callous, Inspector.'

'I'm giving you credit for being good businessmen. With good reason,' Alec said, gesturing round the room. 'What was the voting, as a matter of interest?'

'Five to three. Quite decisive. More or less split on party lines, of course, but that doesn't mean the opposition disagreed on principle.'

'And did you have any idea that your vote might arouse strong feelings in the town?'

'I think they were already aroused, Inspector. The paper in which Tracy appeared does have rather a wide circulation, you know.'

'And it was that pin-up which decided you? Did you know she had done some pictures for a girlie magazine too?'

'I don't recall whether we knew that at the time we made our decision. I rather fancy that came out later. I must say, when I heard about it I did think it was possibly rather unwise of her to get involved with that sort of work.'

'I expect it seemed more glamorous to a young girl than it would to you or me,' Alec said.

'I'm sure you're right. Still, it was rather unpleasant, to think she could bring herself to do it.'

'You knew her, then?'

Richardson hesitated an instant. 'Hardly,' he said. 'Though in a town like this you know everybody to some degree. I've come across her parents in come capacity or another.'

'You didn't know Tracy personally?'

'Personally? Oh no. She was only a teenager, Inspector. I met her when she won the title and at one or two social functions where she was on duty, so to speak. No more than that.'

'Did you think her attractive yourself?' Alec asked casu-

ally. 'You see, I never met her. I wondered whether her
photos did her justice.'

'Oh, you know how it is, Inspector. She had the advan-
tages of youth and good spirits. Make-up and a hairdresser
would do the rest. If you like pretty teenagers, then yes, she
was pretty enough—but you could see a dozen as pretty on
the beach this afternoon.'

'And see as much of them, too,' Alec remarked.

'I'm sorry?'

'I was wondering why, if you prefer to cultivate a slightly
traditional image, you permit toplessness and nude bathing
on your beaches. The Haven does come under the town's
jurisdiction?'

Councillor Richardson smiled easily. 'That's one of the
things I talked of which they bring back from holidays
abroad. We don't like it much, to be honest, but we like less
the idea of the local police patrolling the sands handing out
prosecutions for indecency. I'm sure you appreciate the
dilemma.'

'And the Haven is far enough off to be a case of "out of
sight, out of mind"?'

'Let's say it acts as a safety valve to save the main beaches
from any pressure of that sort. We don't see ourselves as
another Brighton.'

Alec said, 'Do you recall whose idea it was originally, to
strip Tracy of the title?'

'I think it just arose out of general discussion,' Richardson
said. 'I couldn't undertake to say where the idea origin-
ated.'

'You didn't bring it up yourself?'

'Well, really, I doubt it. It was a while before I came to
see that it might be the prudent thing to do.'

'What decided you?'

Richardson looked nonplussed. 'I think—you'll think this
rather quixotic, perhaps—I had an idea it might give Tracy
herself a little jolt, you know. Make her stop and think

whether what she was doing was really in her own best interests.'

The old phrase, thought Alec, the old mask for our selfishness and malice. What cruelties and vengeances could be justified as being in the best interests of the victims? How easily, with that phrase, our vindictiveness is transmuted in our minds into thoughtful kindness.

They sipped their coffee in silence. Alec wondered why Richardson had chosen to meet them in this room. Was he saying, This is my empire, I am a man to beware of? Or did he fancy they would find it harder to make a suspect out of a man who had pleasantly entertained them? Perhaps it was simple good nature, Alec mused hopefully. That was what he had thought at first, until he noticed how Richardson hesitated before answering, and how the warmth in the smile was belied by an increasing chill in the eyes as he pressed his questions.

'It all seems such a shame,' Richardson said. 'The parents must be devastated. Especially coming on top of the unpleasant publicity over her activities. She must have been under more pressure herself than any of us imagined.'

'You think it was suicide?'

'I'm hardly in a position to hold an opinion,' Richardson said, and left the sentence hanging as if inviting Alec to deny or substantiate one theory or another. 'However,' he went on, as Alec remained silent, 'it does seem rather the obvious answer. Young girls are so inclined to emotional upset. As I say, we should hate to think that our decision might have precipitated any sort of crisis, none the less.'

Alec said, 'Suicide is a possibility.'

'I should have thought it had to be.'

'It's a question of how much weight we give certain factors. It certainly would make things simpler for everyone —the parents excepted—if we could show that she took her own life,' Alec said carefully.

Richardson smiled sadly. 'I'm sure you'll arrive at the

wise decision, Inspector. I can see you are a man of percep-
tion.'

Now that Richardson had brought matters to a satisfac-
tory juncture he relaxed and Alec, content with what he had
learnt, rose.

'I can see that being a councillor here is a very delicate
matter,' he said as they took their leave.

'It is,' Richardson said seriously. 'People don't realize the
lengths to which we go to look after their interests. It's a
responsibility.' He brightened, and shook them by the hand.
'It's been a pleasure meeting you, Inspector, despite the sad
circumstances. Anything I can do to help, any doors I can
open, just call. I'll make sure you're always put straight
through to me. Goodbye.'

'Very clever, sir,' Johnson said as he drove back through
the suburbs. 'Letting him think it was evenly balanced. The
question is, why is he so keen for it to be suicide?'

Alec shook his head. 'The question is, rather, why did he
pretend he didn't know Tracy? Because he was pretending,
I'm sure of that. Much better to have told us the truth, or
at least part of it.'

'Perhaps he thinks he's nothing to worry about. On the
face of it, he's right. Why should we connect him with the
death of a teenager on the beach?'

'Mm. Whereas if we didn't believe it before, we now think
he does have some interest in Tracy Ashford's death. I
suppose you picked up the other discrepancy?'

'Sir?'

'Well, it wasn't the picture in the newspaper which caused
the councillors to take the action they did, was it? Think of
the caption. It refers to their action as something that had
already taken place, doesn't it? It laughs at them for being
so puritan. It's conceivable, of course, that the picture was
taken in advance, and the fact that it was to be used was
known to Richardson and the other councillors before it
actually appeared. There is another possibility.'

'It wasn't that picture that triggered things off after all?'

'Precisely. One thing I am sure of. Councillor Richardson's memory is far better than he pretends. It's not that he can't recall the sequence of events. It's that he can, and won't. You'd better do some homework on this, Andy. Check what realy happened in that council meeting. It wouldn't do any harm to get some more information on Mr Richardson, either. There's more to his involvement with Tracy Ashford than meets the eye.'

In the early afternoon Alec and the Superintendent stood on the doorstep of Glamourpix and watched the noisy, litter-strewn street pursue its daily business. From barrows lining the gutters, trilby-hatted vendors touted fruit and vegetables with studious unconcern. They had spotted the two men as policemen, Alec knew, as soon as they had appeared at the street corner. Paper wrappings and cardboard boxes tumbled and shifted in the gusts which eddied up the street, and limp vegetable leaves wrapped themselves lovingly around the kerbstones and the tyres of the cars which threaded their cautious way between the stalls.

Alec turned as footsteps sounded behind the glazed door, and as they drew nearer an amorphous figure enlarged itself behind the frosted glass as on a screen. The door was opened, stuck, and was pulled wider. A girl, or woman, stared languidly at them, a cigarette dangling from her fingers. She wore a baggy purple jumper beneath which was some sort of T-shirt, and tight, short slacks, all seemingly designed to highlight the angularity of the thin shoulders and matchstick limbs. She shrugged without interest and turned back down the passage towards stairs at the far end. Alec stood aside with a dry smile to let the older man enter. Whatever he had expected to find at the end of their journey, it was not this unalluring waif. The glamour of Glamourpix was hardly paraded.

At the top of the stairs they followed the girl down another lino-floored corridor past a grubby kitchen where an electric kettle displayed a perilously frayed flex to their gaze, and a lavatory with a minuscule washbasin attached to the wall. At the far end, the girl pushed a door open with her hips and they followed her into the centre of Glamourpix's operation.

The room was large, high-ceilinged with an ornate cornice, and sunlight filtered dustily through grubby northlights. The sort of room, Alec mused, where the Preraphaelites in their well-off asceticism might have met and painted while Lizzie Siddall pouted on a couch against a backdrop of heavy drapery and significant foliage. And indeed, at the far end of the room just such a couch was set against a wall on a low white dais, an aggressively bright fake tigerskin before it, an ornate cheval mirror behind. The dais was almost enclosed by screens and reflectors, and a battery of lights stood on the yellow pine floorboards. Opposite them, a tubular steel table bore an array of cameras and against it stood a huddle of stands and tripods. Wires snaked across the floor to a row of sockets, from which a thicker cable vanished into a hole in the floor. Over to Alec's right some sort of dressing area had been divided off with a heavy brocade curtain. All this Alec took in in a sweeping glance, before bringing his eyes back to the man who stood scowling before them.

This must be Mervyn Link, Alec guessed, remembering Pringle's note, the man behind Glamourpix and the man who had taken the picture of Tracy which hung on Alec's own office door eighty miles away. Glamourpix, Pringle had said, was not wholly owned by Link but he was the source of such success as it had had—and it was apparently a solid middle-ranker in the strange heirarchy of the glamour photography world. What strange sources Pringle had tapped for his information was a mystery. The last milieu to which Alec would have expected his conventional detective-sergeant to have the *laisser-passer* was this, of the tinsel sex and the glossy fantasy.

'Warm in here, isn't it?' the Superintendent said cheerfully.

''Course it's warm,' Link retorted shortly. 'Think I want a lot of pics of girls with goose pimples?'

'Interrupted you, have we?' The Super gestured towards the lights which shone glaringly on the tigerskin. Link moved to a switch and the lights went out.

'She's dressing,' he said briefly.

'That's a weight off my mind. When she comes out we'll have a little chat, shall we?—' and the big man settled his bulk on a plastic chair. Link bit his lip, then turned to the waif who was leaning against the wall, watching them.

'Fix us some coffee. May as well make a social occasion of it. Seeing as we've got guests.'

The waif lounged out and the three men waited silently while muffled shufflings issued from behind the curtain. After a minute or two the end was pulled back. Alec looked at the girl who emerged with interest and was intrigued to see just such a girl as might be found window-shopping in any London street, or typing letters in an office. She was not tall, but slim, with short chestnut hair neatly cut. The yellow sweatshirt she wore more than hinted at breasts which were full for her build, and her jeans were fashionably clinging. Alec caught the smell of simple, cheap soap, and realized he had been expecting some painted, perfumed glamour model and that instead this girl was no more glamorous than Cathy, or Liz Pink, or any other healthy, attractive young woman.

'Sorry to keep you,' she said. Alec caught a note of amusement in her voice and realized she was aware of his assessment of her. He met her eye and smiled, and saw an answering glint, and she gave a little nod of acknowledgement.

'Martine,' said Link briefly by way of introduction. The two detectives he did not introduce. They sat on the hard plastic chairs in a little semi-circle with the Super as the focus, and sipped the watery coffee which the waif brought in paper cups.

'Tracy Ashford's dead,' the Super said baldly. 'Did you know that?'

'Yeah, we heard. I'm sorry.' Link said it roughly, but looking at him, Alec thought it was probably true. The Super turned to Martine.

'How well did you know her?' he asked curiously.

'It's a small world,' she replied. Her voice was south London, unaffected. 'You get to know most people to chat to, have a drink with. We didn't know her so well, with her not being based in town. She didn't come out with us so much.'

'But she did do so from time to time?'

'Not during the week. Weekends, she drove up sometimes. She'd come out with the crowd of us, sleep on someone's floor, go back Sunday.'

'Where do you go? When you all go out together?'

She shrugged. 'Clubs. You have to make the most of a place like London. It'd be pretty deadly if you didn't.'

'It's an expensive way of having a night out, I should have thought.'

Martine smiled, amused. 'Hardly. A lot of us work in the London clubs, see. So the places out in the suburbs, the country clubs and the like, they love to have us there. You show your card and you're in. Adds a bit of class so far as they're concerned to have a crowd of us there.'

'I'm sure.'

The Superintendent kept the conversation unhurried, unstressed, as it gradually emerged that the world of glamour modelling and the world of the West End gaming clubs and nightclubs were tightly enmeshed, and quite small. The girls who modelled for the magazines worked also as hostesses and croupiers, interspersing periods of office work or agency temping. A life which in the abstract might be quite racy sounded, as Martine described it, strangely normal. Contact with the clients, whether in the clubs or the studios, was marginal so that Martine talked easily of her work although she was, so far as Alec could judge, by no means without modesty of her own. The punters, the men who came to gamble and to be flattered by the provocatively dressed hostesses, interested her hardly at all, just as the photo sessions were divorced entirely from any thought of the downy adolescents and guilty bachelors who were the ultimate clients. What was real was the companionship, the impermanence of the life, the enjoyment of youth and good spirits in a capital city among her friends.

Alec watched Mervyn Link carefully while Martine was speaking, but his expression remained unchanged as she spoke of Tracy Ashford. No doubt dislike of the police was natural to him, but there was no outward indication of any other emotion.

'I think,' the Super said at last, 'it might be as well if we stayed a little longer to chat with Mr Link here.'

Martine took the hint at once. 'I'll pop back later, Merv, shall I? I've some shopping to do anyway.'

Alec rose, forestalling the purple-jumpered waif. 'I'll see you out.'

He led the way down the bleak passage and the steep stairs. At the front door he turned and waited for her to catch him up.

'Sorry we had to interrupt your work,' he said. 'Thanks for being so frank.'

'Sorry I can't be more help. I didn't know her that well.' She paused, eyeing him curiously, and said finally, 'I tell you what, though. If you really want to find out if there's anything else to know, you want to come along one night. Like I said to the other bloke, we're always off somewhere. You might hear something useful.'

Alec said, taken aback, 'Would it go down so well if a policeman tagged along?'

'There's coppers and coppers. And she is dead, after all.

I mean, your lot aren't popular, but you've got to draw the line, haven't you?'

'I suppose you have.'

'Saturday night?'

'Won't you be working?'

'I'm off at nine.'

'Where will you be going?'

'Don't know. Does it matter? I mean, don't come if you don't want to.'

'I'd like to. Thanks for asking.'

'Yeah, well, it's not every bloke I'd ask.' She told him where to come and when, and looked up at him seriously as he reached an arm to open the door.

'We're not all tarts, you know.'

'I know that. And I don't think Tracy was, either. In fact, I think I'd rather have liked to know her.'

The Superintendent glanced at Alec sharply when he returned, then turned to the purple waif. 'Run out and get yourself a sandwich.'

'I don't want a sandwich.'

'Go and see a film, then. See your boyfriend.'

'At this time of day? You must be joking.'

Link turned to her. 'Hop it,' he said briefly. She scowled and ambled out. The Super waited until the sound of her footsteps receded and they heard the front door bang.

'Now, Mr Link,' he said heavily, 'you saw quite a lot of Tracy Ashford in the last couple of months, didn't you? And I don't,' he said, 'mean that as a joke. We're here because she's dead. That's no joking matter. I'll make damn sure the person that killed her won't be laughing, either.'

'It wasn't me.'

'Maybe not. So who was it? Someone you introduced her to? Someone she met in London? Start talking, Mr Link.'

Link sighed. Tracy had come to his studio because a magazine sent her. He did work for them from time to time on a freelance basis. When they approached Tracy after she won the beauty title they had given the job of photographing her to Link. In the event, it was a couple of months before the pictures were used.

'She didn't know much,' Link said. 'Green as they come. But she learned fast and she didn't mind making the effort. Some of these kids, they think modelling's just lounging about in posh clobber. Expect success to drop from heaven on a plate. Tracy was OK to work with. She wasn't too proud to let me tell her how to do it.'

'Shy?' Alec asked. 'About taking her clothes off, I mean.'

'Not so's you'd notice. Not hardened, mind. More like she'd decided it was quite acceptable. With the new girls, it's usually the photographer they're shy of, not the pics. I mean, it's me what they actually have to walk out in front of. She was sensible about that, and we got on well.'

Link, it appeared, had liked working with her well enough to suggest a number of other markets which might be exploited, and it was partly his doing that she had gone to an agent and found herself in demand. It was mixed work. One week she might model earrings, or soap, with only a small part of her body in the shot. Other sessions were more blatantly provocative, like the newspaper pin-up.

'That was the good thing about her. She could do all sorts, not just the beaver shots. She'd have made a living out of it, if she wanted. Not at the top—she wasn't unusual enough for that, if you get me—but there's a good few of the girls who make a nice little income in a quiet way.'

'Leaving the girlie mags behind?'

''Sright. Most of them, that's their level and sooner or later they wake up to the fact. But if you've got it in you to go further, you've got to jack them in. It's all right when you're nobody. They all do it. No one knows, no one cares, except maybe their old granny blows her top. But no one wants the girl that's modelling their thousand quid dresses to be showing her fanny in some girlie mag next week.'

As a result of Link's advice, it seemed that Tracy had

done no more than a couple of the glamour sessions, one
for Link and one for another studio. Link regarded them
balefully. 'You think this job is all dirt. Sure, I do some
glamour pics. What is it, twenty per cent of my work? Less,
probably. Look at that lot over there,' he gestured towards
the table loaded with cameras. 'There's eight thousand
quid's worth of cameras there. I bought another one last
week, matter of fact. Two thousand quid. And that's just
the body. You think that's all built on plain envelopes?'

'Another Lichfield?'

'All right, maybe not. But I do OK. I do good work for
good money.'

'I believe you.' The Superintendent looked at him
thoughtfully. 'Own this lot, do you?'

'It's on long lease,' Link said. 'Fifteen years to run.'

'And the lease, and the posh cameras and whatnot. Mervyn Link owns the whole lot?'

Link's eyes wandered away from the Super's gaze while
he thought about his answer.

'You do own some of it, I suppose?'

'Two-thirds. Two-thirds is mine.'

'And the other third?'

'One of these leisure groups. You know. They run some
clubs, publish some mags. They came in a year or so back.
I don't remember exactly.' He gave them the name.

'Have trouble with the lease, did you?'

Link looked at him and nodded. 'Rent review.'

'And now they send you work, and you send them a share
in the profits.'

'Right.'

'What else do you send them, Mr Link? Girls? For their
parties, for escorting good customers? To help out in the
clubs?'

'What do you think this is, white slaving? You've been
reading too many cheap books, copper. The clubs are big
business, and they're legit, too. Like the pics.'

'So you never send girls along to make up the numbers at a party and earn themselves a useful little present at the same time?'

'I might do.'

'Tracy Ashford?'

'Maybe.'

'Yes or no?'

'All right, yes. Once. Some Arab wanted to throw a party at one of the clubs. They needed some girls to make the numbers up, help it go with a swing. I mentioned it to one or two. Tracy, yes.'

'Did she go?'

'How do I know?'

'How about Martine?' Alec asked. Link's head turned towards him speculatively. 'Was she one of the ones who helped it go with a swing?'

'Maybe. I don't recall. They work their own grapevine.'

'We'll have a word with your business partners, Mr Link,' the Superintendent said. 'Would you like to tell us before we go, just as a matter of routine, where you were on Tuesday this week?'

Link smiled viciously. 'I don't mind at all, copper. As it happens, I was taking pics for a coffee commercial.'

'Here?'

'No. On top of Blackpool Tower. If you want to check, there was about fifty blokes up there with me. All right?'

'Fine.' The Super got to his feet, equable still. 'I'm sorry we've had to interrupt your day's work, Mr Link. Perhaps we'll be in touch again. We'll see ourselves out.'

But Mervyn Link followed them out of the room and down to the frosted glass door, and when they were outside he stood on the step and watched them all the way down the vegetable-strewn street. As they turned the corner Alec looked back. Mervyn Link stood there still, among the shouting barrow boys and the bustling shoppers, watching them, unmoving.

As they descended the stairs to the underground car park Alec told the Superintendent of his brief conversation with Martine, and her unexpected offer.

'Hm. As you say, it's too useful to pass up. I don't suppose some of her friends will like it, all the same. Think it's straight?'

'I think so, sir. So far as one can tell. I'll try and keep my wits about me.'

'You'd better. The last thing I can do with is a scandal about one of my officers in goings-on in some nightclub. I wish someone could go with you, but that's out, of course. All right. Just watch your step.'

'I'll get Johnson or Pringle to follow up about this party Link mentioned, sir, try and establish whether Tracy actually went and who she might have met there. They can do some work on Link's business partners, too.'

'All right. But, Alec, when you know who they are, tread warily. I'd rather make any contact myself, in fact. With some of these organizations, the clubs and the girlie mags are the good side. Behind it there may be things which are a lot less pleasant. And interests a lot more powerful.'

'The sort of interests which wouldn't allow anyone to stand in their way?' Alec asked with a sharp glance.

'Yes,' the Superintendent said heavily. 'That's exactly what I mean.'

CHAPTER 6

It was late in the afternoon by the time Alec returned to the cramped police station, still turning over in his mind the implications of what they had learnt at Mervyn Link's studio. The case had opened out from the dusty little resort, and he was apprehensive about the possibility of losing the thread of the investigation in the byways and cul-de-sacs of the capital. It was easy to contemplate the prospect of dealing with suspects like Henderson or Councillor Richardson, but London club bosses lived in a different world altogether, where the criminal wore the pinstripe suit of the businessman, and had power and money to enforce his designs—and also, perhaps, had as good a brain as Alec's own, or better. Success was no foregone conclusion in a case where such men were involved.

Alec started to sort through his notes, but it was only minutes after he had sat at his desk that the first interruption came. Liz Pink knocked at the door and came in at his call, bearing coffee and a slab of cake.

'Thought you might be in need of these, sir,' she said, watching him anxiously. Alec smiled. 'Thanks. You anticipate my every whim.'

She relaxed and said, 'I've arranged for you to see the students Tracy shared with, sir, this evening. I can put them off if you'd rather.'

'No, keep it. I want you along yourself, too, if you please.'

'Fine, sir. I arranged it for eight.' Alec glanced at the clock on the wall. It was five-thirty. 'And Detective-Sergeant Pringle wants a word when he comes off the phone, sir. And DC Johnson's outside too.'

'I see. They sent you in as envoy to test the waters, did they, Liz?'

She blushed and said, 'Shall I say you'll see them?'

'Send them in.'

Andy Johnson had spent the afternoon reading through council minutes and talking to the leader of the council's opposition group. He had been able to confirm the facts as Richardson had given them of the council committee meeting where the decision had been taken to remove Tracy's title.

'It seems the idea didn't come from Richardson, sir. But that may not mean he didn't plant it for one of his supporters to bring up. This chap says the vote was along party lines, but he got the impression some of Richardson's group weren't too enthusiastic about it. It sounded a little vindictive, maybe, and the arguments about the town's image weren't too overwhelming. There was one old boy, however, who apparently sees red over matters of this sort, and he carried a certain amount of opinion with him. Seems he's still regretting the passing of the bathing machine. As to the dates, the committee made their decision after the paper had had the picture taken, but in time for the caption to be concocted referring to what they'd done. The same councillor who introduced the motion told the committee that the pin-up was going to appear, and they took his word for it.'

'No other pictures of her appeared around that time?'

'Actually, yes. She was featured in a three-page spread in a girlie magazine two weeks before. My informant says this wasn't referred to at the committee meeting, and indeed he wasn't aware of it until it came out in the general muckraking later. I spent some time in the library looking up back numbers of the local paper. Letters were pretty evenly balanced, but there was a leader which came out in favour of what the council had done. So far as Tracy's own mail goes, her parents weren't really very helpful. If Tracy did have any hate mail, she seems to have kept it from them.'

Alec nodded. It was all routine, unexciting stuff. 'Like to go and see the councillor who raised the motion? See if you can find out if there were other interests behind him. Take another officer with you. I shouldn't expect any dramatic revelations, Andy, but it all helps build up the picture.'

Johnson went out, and a moment later Pringle took his place. As soon as he entered, Alec could see he was elated.

'You look like you've just caught a murderer, John. I take it it's good news.'

'Right, sir. One, we've found out who the showman is that Tracy chummed up with.' He referred to his notebook. 'He's James Alexander White, known to his friends as Jumbo. Aged twenty-six, and he's been coming here every summer season since he was sixteen. He runs an amusement arcade on the pier, sir. Three or four of Tracy's schoolfriends confirm that she palled up with him. They thought it an odd friendship, because it seems this White is the opposite of Tracy in many ways—rather an odd character, and not outgoing at all. Still, apparently Tracy liked him and saw a lot of him.'

'Was she doing so still? Or had it died the death as she grew older?'

'Don't know, sir, to be honest; White could tell us, of course, but I reckoned you'd want to tackle him, so I left him alone. I did check that he's here this summer, though, and that he hasn't run away.'

'Good. We'll go and see him.'

'There's another lead that looks more promising, sir. I've tracked down that doctor who used to work at the health centre here. The thing is, he's done a bunk.'

Alec sat up. 'Has he, now? That *is* interesting.'

'Even more so when you learn that he pushed off on Wednesday morning, without leaving a forwarding address. His partners are pretty fed up with him. They've rather been left in the lurch.'

'I fancy this calls for a man on the spot. Like a trip to the Midlands, John? You know the people to see. Find out if he went by car—'

'I've already put out a search for it, sir.'

'Good man. I want him found, John. And I'd give a lot to know whether he knew Tracy's death was being treated as murder before he went. And how he heard of it in the first place.'

'Yes, sir. But that's not quite all.'

'Spit it out.'

'Ricchi wasn't at work on Tuesday at all. He was on call from home until nine a.m., when he rang the surgery to hand over. That's the last time they spoke to him. If you allow him three hours for the journey, sir, he could still have been here just after midday. He could easily have met Tracy in her lunch-hour. He could have killed her.'

Dawn Mills sat tearfully on a battered settee, a plain girl whom happiness or passion might have rendered attractive, now merely drained and very young. Beside her, protectively, sat Darryl Norton, while the third of the trio, Robert Tomkins, squatted athletically on a battered dining chair. The three teenagers displayed a sullen, unpractised resentment which emphasized their youth and immaturity in contrast with the control and self-possession of the twenty-five-year-old Liz Pink.

Alec made his voice even, unthreatening, to dispel the idea of 'sides' before it had consciously arisen in their minds. 'It's awful when your friends die,' he said. 'When it happened to me, I'd never come across death at all. Then a friend of mine killed himself in a car while we were still at school. It had never occurred to me, I don't think, that we were subject to death just like other people.'

There was no response. This was preamble, and the three teenagers waited sullenly for something more to the point.

'I've got to investigate Tracy's death,' Alec went on. 'I expect you know by now that it's unlikely that she died by accident. As a matter of interest, was she a good swimmer?'

'Not bad.' Darryl's reply was curt, reluctant.

'That's what we thought,' Alec said, nodding. 'Beyond that, obviously, there are the possibilities of suicide or of murder. That sounds terribly dramatic, but I'm afraid murder does actually happen, and if it happened to Tracy then I have to do everything I can to make sure it doesn't happen to anybody else.' He hesitated. 'I like Tracy,' he said. 'I don't mean that I ever met her. But I get to know people almost better than their friends when I have an investigation like this to do. It might help you to realize that I do really want to help.'

'If you say so,' Robert Tomkins said. 'Not many people

of your generation were that fond of Tracy.'

Alec winced at the sweeping classification, and said, 'Because they don't like younger people in general? Or didn't like her in particular?'

'They all took her mum and dad's side.'

'I suppose,' Alec said, 'they all thought you were living a life of wild parties, drugs and so forth.'

'Of course they did,' Darryl said. 'Stands to reason, doesn't it? If we share a house we must all be promiscuous. We're the younger generation. We're responsible for junkies, and AIDS and vandalism.'

'They're the ones who brought it all about,' Dawn said. 'But what do we hear? It's all the younger generation this, and the younger generation that. Making us the scapegoats for their own mistakes.'

'And when Tracy began her modelling career,' Alec suggested, 'it must have added fuel to the fire.'

The three teenagers looked at each other, and Alec realized that they too had found it hard to come to terms with Tracy's actions. He said as much, and Robert nodded. 'We wouldn't try and prevent her, but we were a bit puzzled. Why should she do rubbish?'

'Why indeed?' Alec said. 'It seemed out of character, so far as I can find out. Did you decide what made her do it?'

'Not really. I guess she thought it would lead to something better.'

Dawn said, 'I don't think she cared. Her body was something she could use as she pleased. It wasn't sacred, and if she could make a bit of money out of it without too much hassle, why not?' She bit her lip at her own outspokenness, and subsided into the settee again. Alec thought she was probably pretty near the mark.

Aloud, he said, 'But she wasn't short of money? To the rest of you she must have seemed quite well off.'

Dawn shrugged. 'You can always use more.'

Alec said, 'Someone suggested that she didn't actually enjoy the modelling very much. Is that true?'

Again, it was Dawn who answered, as if the boys accepted that they had no writ to enter the territory of female emotion. 'It could have have been someone she met, who got under her skin. She used to go up to London occasionally, apart from the modelling.'

'Someone a little too pressing? Someone she didn't take to but had to put up with for the sake of business?'

'Something like that.'

Over in the corner by the window, Liz Pink shifted in her seat. The evening sun was still warm, and her uniform skirt, unsuitable for the heat, clung unflatteringly. It would do her no harm to lose some more weight, she thought.

'Will you tell me about Tracy's relationships?' Alec said. 'Did you know any of her boyfriends? Did she bring them here?'

There was a silence as none of them leapt to answer. 'What about the doctor?' Alec prompted. 'What about him?'

'Nothing much to say.' Robert shrugged. 'He came here a bit. We didn't get to know him well.'

'Stayed the night?'

'Sure.' A note of hostility crept into his voice.

'When he moved away they split up, of course?'

'Yes. He was a bit too keen on Tracy for her liking, so I think she wasn't sorry when circumstances brought it to an end.'

'Did he take it badly?'

'Dunno. We never saw him again.'

'Yes we did,' Dawn said unexpectedly. 'I did, anyway.'

Robert looked at her for explanation, and she said, 'He came here one Saturday when you were out. He was acting a bit wet, and I was glad when he went.'

'Wet?' Alec echoed. 'Still soft on Tracy, you mean?'

'Mm. How badly she'd treated him, but at the same time

how everything could be wonderful if they could only get together again. Could I put a word in for him? Embarrassing.'

'You never said,' Robert said.'

'Didn't I?'

'And nobody else was here. Tracy was out?'

'She was in town—in London. He was crazy to see her. He'd driven down that afternoon specially, said he'd told her in his last letter that he would, so he wasn't very happy that she was in London.'

'Did you tell him where she was?'

'So far as I knew. I mean, she sometimes said they were going to some club or hotel, but as often she just went.'

'What had she said this time? Think back. What did you actually tell Ricchi when he pressed you?'

Dawn pursed her lips in a pantomime of anxious thought. 'I think she said something about a country club. Near Bromley. I remember I couldn't be very precise.'

'And that satisfied him?'

'Hardly. But he left all the same. I was jolly glad. I didn't want him here all evening telling me how wonderful Tracy was.'

'Was he going to drive home again?'

'I don't think so.' The effort to remember puckered her brow. 'I think he said something like "How on earth will I find her?" As if he was going to try.'

Alec said, 'Can you remember when this would have been?'

She shook her head. 'I don't know.'

'And you don't know whether Ricchi ever found her that night? Did he come here again?'

All three shook their heads.

'Did Tracy seem particularly agitated when she came back that weekend?'

'How on earth can I remember that?' Dawn complained.

Alec smiled. 'Fair enough. But look, will you try and

pin down which weekend it was? Use something else as a reference. Will you?'

Dawn agreed, reluctantly, to try. Alec asked about other friends of Tracy's, but there was little they could tell him. Yes, sometimes she had brought people back, but Alec gained the impression that Ricchi was the only serious attachment. He asked about Willie Henderson, but it was clear that they viewed him as no more than a hanger-on, a relic of Tracy's schooldays.

Alec looked at the two boys. 'Neither of you . . .?' Both shook their heads. He looked for hesitations, flushes of guilt, and saw none. 'She was a very attractive girl,' he said tentatively.

'It's not like that,' Darryl said. 'We shared a house, that's all, for God's sake.'

'To be more honest,' Robert added, 'she liked men a little older. That's why Henderson was never in the running— plus he was too provincial, of course, just as we were.'

'Tracy preferred a degree of sophistication? Or just older men?'

'Not that much older. Not the old rams who bothered her when she won the title. They were just ridiculous.'

'Disgusting,' Dawn said.

'She got attentions she didn't fancy?' Alec asked.

'Oh, sure. Especially after she started modelling. It proved for them she was some sort of tart. They took her title off her in public, and at the same time started to treat her as some sort of available prostitute.'

'They?'

'The old men. The worthies. Councillors. Retired judges. You know the sort. This place is stiff with them.'

'I'd be interested to know whether there was one, more than the others, who treated her that way,' Alec said carefully, but the import of his question seemed to pass them by as they looked at each other, refreshing their memories.

'No one special,' Darryl said.

'There was Richardson,' Dawn said.

'Richardson?'

Dawn turned to Alec. 'He's a bloke who runs a plastic gnome factory. Well, plastics, anyway. Gnomes would be about his mark. He's a big wheel on the council. He took Trace out to dinner before they took her title off her. She thought it was a bit of a joke, but when she came back she was furious. Seems all he wanted to do was give her a cheap meal, then drive her up on to the downs for a quick feel. She always believed, after that, that he was the one who had put the rest of them up to it. Said it would be just like his hypocrisy.'

'Did he get what he wanted? Up on the downs, I mean.'

'I doubt it. Tracy might have let him have a grope if she felt sorry for him, but the way she was talking when she got back it sounded as if they'd had a real fight. She'd been all set to walk back, though in the end he drove her.'

'Did she say any more about it?'

'Only the next day. She said something about him still being sore. I mean—' she flushed and looked round at Liz briefly—'I think she'd done something to, well, cool his ardour for him.'

'I think I understand,' said Alec with a ghost of a smile. 'Though it doesn't sound as if he deserves much sympathy for that.'

Robert, who had been following the conversation with anxiety increasingly written in his face, said, 'But you can't think that he'd actually . . .'

'Somebody did,' Alec said soberly, 'unless she committed suicide. But for the moment I think I'd rather you didn't put two and two together. In fact, I'd rather you said nothing about my visit at present. Talk about it among yourselves, by all means, and if you find that jogs your memory about something which might be relevant, let me know straight away. But so far as other people go, keep quiet. Do you think you can do that?'

'I guess so.' Robert looked round at the others, and nodded. 'We'll say nothing.'

They saw them to the door in silence, and Alec said a brief goodbye. He and Liz stood on the steps for a moment, looking down the valley to the glitter of the sea. This part of the town was quiet. Apart from the distant hum of traffic, it could have been a Sunday.

'I didn't like Councillor Richardson much, when I met him,' Alec said meditatively. He glanced sideways at Liz Pink, weary and perspiring at his side. 'It seems my instincts were not altogether wrong. Come on. Let's get back.'

They walked back down to the police station, each wrapped in their own thoughts. For Alec's part, they were thoughts of Richardson's role in Tracy Ashford's life, and the motive for his lie about not knowing the dead girl. Surely he must have realized that these things could be checked? If their intimacy had been limited to the one occasion, however, it was quite possible that Richardson had extracted some promise of silence from Tracy, or fancied he had. Alec was pretty sure that whatever attraction Richardson had felt to the girl had been changed to malice by his treatment at her hands. Men of his type didn't take kindly to humiliation. Yet it was difficult to see that malice being carried to the point of murder unless there were other factors Alec was not aware of. For example, had Richardson known that Tracy was modelling for glamour magazines? Was he a devotee of such works himself? Or had he some other contact with that seedy world?

Then again, for murder to have occurred, there had to be occasion for it, and that implied that it was Richardson for whom Tracy had dressed so provocatively on that last day of her life, and that she planned to meet him on the beach in her lunch-break. How, though, could Richardson manage to lure her into the water, minus all her clothes, and drown her? The thought of a friendly bathe together was hardly consistent with Tracy's anger at his earlier rudeness, and she had been an athletic girl, whom it would have been no easy task to subdue.

They reached the town square, and he glanced at his watch. There was still time, if he was not too long about sorting out the day's paperwork, to call and see Cathy and Heather. He wanted to explain that he would be away on Saturday night, and he must warn Miss Helston and Miss Hanson at the hotel, too.

'You'd better get off,' he said to Liz as they climbed the steps. 'I'll be in trouble if I start allowing you to tot up too much overtime. Besides, I'm sure you want to get off. It's no fun working late on a Friday night.'

'That doesn't matter, sir,' Liz lied. On the walk down through the town her own thoughts had been of the difficulty of getting her boyfriend to understand that she just couldn't anticipate when she might be able to see him while a murder inquiry was in train. He really showed himself to be ridiculous with his persistent complaining about her work. The more he went on in that way, the less likely it was that she would want to see him anyway. It was no relaxation, to listen to his whines. Well, there was time this evening, if she signed off smartly, to spend an hour or two together. She would ring him from the station, if Inspector Farmer wasn't about. She was beginning to think that in the long term, though, the boyfriend would have to go. Possessiveness was something she just could not stand. The trouble was, how did you meet people in a place like this? It was just so limited. No wonder Tracy Ashford had flown to London like a bird released from its cage when the opportunity arose.

It was half past ten when Alec gained the comfort of the Logan Hotel. In the lounge, the Captain was playing bezique with Miss Helston, while a family from Leeds sat demurely in a corner, leafing through magazines. Alex explained to Miss Helston that he would be absent on Saturday night—he intended to stay over at his parents' home, if indeed his London outing finished before daylight. He would pay for the room, naturally, and would be back on Sunday.

Miss Helston smiled. Of course that would be all right. Could she make him some sandwiches for his journey? The Captain watched suspiciously, his eyes bulging in their sockets, resenting the interruption and obviously unsure whether he should be on speaking terms with this young man who indulged in such odd goings-on. The idea of a business trip to London, in the middle of a holiday, on a Saturday night, sounded fishy to him, decidedly fishy. Probably the boy was up to no good. He wouldn't be surprised at all if it was to do with drugs. The Captain had heard that the south coast resorts were rife with the stuff. Pity the police hadn't locked the fellow up when they had the chance. He glanced at his cards as Miss Helston resumed her place, drew out four and laid them face up on the table.

'Double bezique, ma'am, I'm sorry to say. My game, I fancy.'

There was life in the old dog yet.

CHAPTER 7

It was as well that Alec slept well on Friday night, for Saturday morning brought a rush of work which had him juggling madly with the limited resources at his disposal. The disappearance of Guy Ricchi from his Midlands surgery was too coincidental by far to be neglected, and Alec judged that it was worth sending Pringle to follow it up on the spot, even though his absence would be sorely felt. At present, Ricchi's actions made him far the likeliest suspect in the inquiry, but there were too many imponderables involved, and until they located the man himself they were no further forward.

The amusement arcade proprietor, Jumbo White, had to

be interviewed, and Alec arranged to take Johnson with him that afternoon down on to the pier. Meanwhile, there was the routine of checking whereabouts and alibis to be covered. Councillor Richardson, in view of his more intimate connection with the dead girl, would have to be seen again—and there was the question of Mervyn Link and his shadowy partners, who might or might not have employed Tracy as hostess in their gambling parties. Alec contemplated the list of tasks and the list of personnel and knew that something would have to give, and in this case it would be the time schedule. Everything would move more slowly, that was all, and if there was a risk that some vital factor would be concealed before they reached it, why, that was a risk that he had no option but to take. He contemplated his outing to London, planned for that evening, and reluctantly decided that he would have to go through with it. It was unlikely, maybe, to be fruitful, but it was a chance, and one that he could not expect to be offered again.

At midday Detective-Sergeant Pringle rang from the Midlands, but only to confirm what they already knew. Ricchi had had Tuesday, the day Tracy died, free, and first indications were that he had been absent from the town all day. On the Wednesday, without warning, he had rung his partners and told them he could not do his day's work, and within the hour he had left his digs by car. Pringle was about to interview the young engineer Ricchi had shared the digs with. If necessary, did Alec want to arrange for a search warrant to be obtained? Alec confirmed that he did. There was no way that Ricchi's actions could be seen as anything but highly suspicious. If his digs contained any indication of his involvement with Tracy, or his present whereabouts, the sooner they could find it the better.

Forty minutes later, after a snatched ham roll and yet another cup of coffee, Alec and Johnson set out for the seafront once more.

*

It was not hard to see why the name Jumbo had clung to James White. Physically large, he wore the baggiest of jeans, which sagged in folds around his ankles and at the seat, and his face, too, had the sad, ponderous expression of an elephant. By coincidence, or in unconscious self-parody, he had acquired the mannerism of swaying his large head from side to side, as if waving a trunk in search of buns, and he was doing so now as they sat in the back room behind the amusement arcade on the pier's lower deck. Overhead, feet echoed on the boarding, while from somewhere beneath the salty tang of the sea arose from the waves which soughed among the pier legs. The room was built for business, not for pleasure. Tiny, dirty windows of thick glass gave the only view of the outside world, but on the inner wall were a number of windows of one-way glass through which Jumbo White could watch proceedings in the arcade. A worn oak table and two benches formed the bulk of the furniture, with two shabby filing cabinets, but a substantial safe, firmly bolted through the planking, hinted that this might be no dead-end business.

Alec said directly, 'You'll have heard by now that Tracy Ashford is dead, Mr White. You must be upset by that, because I understand you knew her well.'

'Yeah?' Jumbo's voice was hoarse, uncooperative.

'Isn't that true?'

'If it is, it ain't none of your business.'

'It has to be my business,' Alec said quietly. 'Don't you think it's important to find out how she died, and why? If I said it's possible somebody killed her, don't you think it's my business, and yours too, to do everything we can to find out who?'

White's head waved slowly from side to side as he deliberated. 'All right,' he said at length. 'I knew her.'

'Well?'

'Well enough.'

'You'll have to tell me a little more than that. How long

had you known her? How often did you see her?'

'You ask a lot of questions, copper. I've known her three years. Maybe four. I come down 'ere in the summer, see, to run the shows.'

'Are they yours?'

'Well, not to say mine exclusively. We got shows at Yarmuff an' Weston, an' Skeggie. Me bruvver looks arter Weston, an' me old man an' the old lady does Yarmuff an' Skeggie between 'em. I do 'ere.'

'Do they make a good profit?' Alec asked interestedly. Jumbo shrugged, and said nothing.

Alec said, 'How did you meet Tracy?'

'She come to play the machines, wiv 'er mates from school. When she was fifteen or so. Well, she runs out of change, doesn't she, and as there's a sign up there what everyone can see which says you can't ask for change but has to get it outer the change machine, she comes up to me, all cheeky, and asks for some. An' we sort of got chatting. And then she comes again the next day, and the same thing happens. Soon we started to go out places together in the mornings when the shows were quiet, and in the evenings she'd come an' help behind the counter.'

'Did you sleep with her?'

Jumbo looked offended. 'I did not. For starters, she was under age, wasn't she?'

'Not for long,' Alec observed. 'She was a very good-looking girl. It wouldn't be so surprising if you had become lovers.'

He refrained from saying that she had slept with other men. White must know that.

'Well, we didn't,' Jumbo said sulkily. Alec wondered if he was lying, and decided he couldn't tell.

'And you took up your friendship each year, as it were, when you came down for the season?'

'Yeah, well last summer she took up wiv some other bloke what worked at the 'ealph centre, so she didn't come down here no more, or not so much, after that.'

'And then, she was concentrating on her modelling career, too.'

White got heavily to his feet and wandered to one of the viewing windows, and peered through. Alec said, 'Did you like it much, when she started that?'

'None of my business, was it?' White replied, his face averted. 'It wasn't for me to like it or not like it.'

'Are you saying you had no feelings about it at all? Come on, Mr White. You know the sort of magazines we're talking about. Did you really feel nothing either way when you found your mates sniggering over a picture of her with her legs apart?'

Jumbo White turned on him with a snarl. 'Just watch what you say, copper. You're trying to make Trace out to be some kind of tart, encha? You ever meet 'er? No, of course you ain't.'

'If she wasn't a tart, why did she do tart's work?' Alec said brutally, and a stab of guilt as he remembered Martine made his voice harsher still.

'OK, she done it. I don't know why. But she weren't no tart, an' that's all there is to it, so you can write that in your little book, copper,' he added viciously, turning to Johnson, 'and stuff it where the monkey put the nuts.'

Alec nodded towards the viewing windows. 'Which of the shows makes the most money?'

White eyed him suspiciously, but some of the aggression left him none the less. 'The machines make a good deal,' he said grudgingly. 'They all play them, see? The kids, the 'ousewives, the grannies, everyone. It's frewput what does it. The novelties, the peepshows an' what 'ave you, they don't make much. But you gotter ave 'em, on a pier, encha? ''Swhat people expect.'

'With four arcades, your family must do quite comfortably.'

'It ain't all jam, copper, believe me. Take out the 'ire of

the machines, the rent of the space, rates, bloody tax. There's not much left, I tell yer.'

'And you have to spend every day here, in the season?'

'Have to. Them kids what's out the front taking the money, I'd as soon trust them wiv me kid sister as wiv the dough. You gotter keep on the ball. There's machines start to go up the spout. It ain't no way to make money if they start to cough up too much prizes.'

'The day Tracy died, for instance. You were here then?'

'What day was that?' White asked aggressively.

'You don't know? It was in all the papers.'

'Reading the papers ain't something I does a lot of. Sure I knew she was dead. That don't mean I was leaning over the pier watching when they pulled her out.'

'Out of where?'

'Out of the sea,' Jumbo said with sarcasm. 'Where do you think they pulled her out of? An 'at?'

'You took a fair amount of notice of what was said, if you know they pulled her out within sight of the pier. But you don't know which day it was?'

'You can see the 'ole bloody beach from the pier. All right, Wednesday, was it?'

'Tuesday. So where were you?'

'Here,' he said triumphantly. 'All day, from 'arf nine till midnight. All blooming day. Ask the kids out front.'

'I will. Fourteen and a half hours. That's a long time. You stayed on the pier all day?'

'Ain't I just said so? Got me lunch off of Benny's fish an' chip restaurant up top, an' me tea, too. Chap from the council came, that was Tuesday, about free pee em. Fire precautions, or escape precautions, or some bleeding precautions. 'E 'ad time to spend 'arf the day on them, anyhow.' Jumbo White hesitated, his large head questing from side to side as if the answer to his problem was lying on the floor somewhere waiting to be picked up. 'That was after Trace had been in.'

'You saw her? You saw Tracy on the day she died?'

'Must've done, if it was Tuesday. Only, if she hadn't gone an' got 'erself killed I wouldn't've said. She told me not to say nuffink.'

'Why did she do that?'

'She was going to see some bloke, that's why, what'd been bothering 'er. An' she didn't want no nosey parkers putting two and two together an' making five. She called to see me on the way. Don't suppose she was 'ere more than ten minutes.'

'Who was this man she was going to see, Mr White?'

He shrugged. 'Dunno, do I? You're the copper. Can't you find out?'

'It'd be easier if you could tell me.' But Jumbo merely stared at him impassively. Alec said, 'Anyway, it was nice of her to call in. What was she wearing?'

'Eh? Wearing? Some sort of skirt. What do you mean, what was she wearing?'

'I just wondered if she was wearing anything particularly memorable.'

'Not that I remember.'

'Had you seen her often, this summer?'

'Nah. She'd took up wiv other blokes. She popped along, though, from time to time to see how I was getting along. She was a good sort, was Trace.'

'I believe she was. Look, Mr White, you realize that what you're saying is important. You saw Tracy only a few hours before her body was pulled from the sea. All you can say is that she was going to meet someone else when she left you?'

''Sright.'

'Do you know where? Did she say?'

'She didn't say, and I didn't ask her.'

'Did you form the impression it was a meeting she was looking forward to? Was she keyed up?'

'Well, I dunno. She was a bit keyed up, like. She was going to tell this bloke where he got off.'

'What did she say that gave you that impression?'

But Jumbo White could not, or would not, recall. Alec asked a few more questions, then glanced at Johnson and got to his feet.

'Thanks for your time, Mr White. We'll want you to make a formal statement at some stage. You won't like that much, but it has to be done. In the meantime, if you remember anything else—anything at all—of what Tracy said or did or planned that last day of her life, you'll come and say, won't you? You owe her that, at least.'

'Yeah.'

They left him standing in the long, bleak room and went out into the arcade. A handful of youngsters were dedicatedly playing computer attack games, pooling their money. Two or three tourists ambled slowly through.

'Have a word with these lads,' Alec said, gesturing to the youths who lounged behind the pay desks and the electronic bingo. 'Just see if they can back up White's story at all. Don't get too heavy.'

Johnson nodded and made for the nearest counter. Alec looked round, spotted the viewing window with its one-way glass and sketched a smile for Jumbo White's benefit. Then he wandered over to the shooting gallery and picked up one of the little rifles. It was clean, and well cared for.

'I'll be wasting my money on this,' he said to the boy behind the counter. 'Let me have a pound's worth.'

'Depends how good a shot you are,' the boy said. 'There's nothing wrong with the guns. Might make more money if there was.'

Alec paid his pound, and the boy broke the little gun, cocked it and handed it to him. He pressed a button, and bright yellow ducks began to sail rather fast across the gaudy background among painted targets and outlines of tanks. A tiny battledressed figure popped up and a light flashed as it fired at Alec before disappearing again.

'They're the most points,' the lad said. 'The men.'

Alec laid the rifle along his cheek, his elbows comfortably apart on the counter, and waited for another minute soldier to spring up. The rifle cracked, and the man disappeared.

'You've used one of these before,' the boy said.

'Not one of these,' Alec said, thinking of the many weapons he had cuddled to him over the years, and the targets he had had in his sights. 'Something like it, though.'

He took the second rifle from the boy and followed one of the gaudy ducks along its mechanical track, knocking it down just before it passed behind the backing. He handed the gun back. 'You'll lose money on this stall.'

'That's what I said,' the boy answered, handing Alec a fluffy dog as his prize. 'He takes too much care of those guns. Can't abide them not shooting straight. A place like this ought to have an element of chance in it, or where are you?'

'Is he like that with all the stalls?'

'Only the guns. The others he runs pretty sharpish. He and his family, they spend every winter in the Bahamas. At least, that's what we heard. Only, he's got this thing about guns. When he's had a few, or if you've done something good, as a reward, like, he'll show you his collection. All rare ones. Real guns. He's got a German Luger that used to be owned personally by Rommel. At least,' the boy added, 'that's what he says.'

Alec asked about the previous Tuesday, but there was nothing the boy could recollect about the day except his regret at not being down on the beach to see the dead girl pulled from the water. Certainly, he could remember none of the visitors to the amusement arcade that day. Nor could he remember whether White had been there all day, although he confirmed that he usually was. Alec nodded and left, the fluffy dog under his arm.

They came out on to the open decking of the pier and walked back towards the beach. 'Anything useful?' Alec asked.

'One of them saw the girl, sir. He's a local lad, and he knew who she was, and remembered her calling before. He puts the time at between one and two. Saw her playing one of the computer games, but things were busy then so he doesn't know what happened to her after that.'

Alec said, 'I got a fluffy dog for my trouble, and the information that White's got a thing about guns. The rifles in the shooting gallery are spotless and he's apparently got a private collection. Better check that out when we get back, see what he's got a licence for.'

'It doesn't get us a lot further forward, though, does it, sir? Tracy was drowned, not shot.'

'True. And White says he was on the pier all day.'

'That's corroborated by one of the lads, sir. He could have nipped off when he was getting his fish and chips, though, couldn't he?'

'He could. Of course, if he and this Benny in the fish restaurant are chums, that's going to be difficult to check. Assuming his story is true, though, who was the man Tracy was going to meet? She was going to teach him a lesson. White spotted that, and so did the woman at the surgery, Miss Buxted.'

They reached the pier gates and stood on the promenade gazing back at the pavilion at the far end. 'He could have pushed her off it,' Johnson said, not very hopefully.

'She was held under water.' Alec turned and looked along the promenade towards the headland. 'Got a minute? Let's take a walk along, Andy. Take a note of the time and let's see how long it takes us to get up on to the headland.' He shaded his eyes, and caught the glint of the sun on metal on the skyline. 'We'll go as far as that car park and see what we can see.'

It was difficult to make any sort of speed along the promenade; after a few hundred yards Alex unloaded the furry dog into the arms of a bewildered six-year-old and gradually they neared the far end and the crowds thinned out. The path forked, one part descending to the undercliff walk which finished in a viewpoint, the other climbing past Cathy and Heather's apartment, more and more steeply up the side of the downs. The houses receded and they came out on to the open side of the headland, where fathers flew kites in the updraught and children looked on doubtfully. Alec stopped to let them get their breath and they looked back at the yellow beach dotted with colour, the cars flashing along the front, the glittering pier stretching out over the sea, where Jumbo White presided over his toffee apples and fruit machines, his bingo and his beloved guns. They turned and pressed on over the short turf. The curve of the headland hid the summit until the last moment, and they came out suddenly into a roughly surfaced car park, where they were eyed suspiciously by elderly couples sitting close to their cars. A low lavatory block, spray painted by vandals, squatted to one side. The edge of the cliff, unfenced, was a hundred yards off. Beyond, out to sea, coasters shimmered and a ferry drew its shining wake towards France.

'Twenty minutes, sir.'

'And twenty back. Say another ten minutes each way from the health centre to the pier. Doesn't leave much time, does it, even out of a two-hour lunch-break. Yet she took the time to walk along the pier and see her old friend Jumbo White.'

'Maybe she was early for her appointment. She could still have had three-quarters of an hour here, if it was here she came. More, if she went back by a more direct route.'

'It's a tempting rendezvous, especially with someone coming by car. You could talk in reasonable privacy. Plenty of people about to prevent anything unpleasant happening, but all tourists so no one would recognize them.'

'But how do you get her from here into the sea? Over the edge of the cliff?'

'Hardly. The post-mortem would have shown that up, I should have thought. And it's too crowded here for an

abduction against her will. Though people are pretty pass-
ive. It might have been done.' He looked at his watch. 'We
ought to be getting back, by rights. What do you say,
though, to going on into the next bay?'

'The Haven? Sure.'

'Could you take a car down there?'

'Not by a direct road. From here, you'd have to go back
inland, turn west along the main road and then turn off
again. But it's little more than a track, two or three miles
long. That's what keeps the place relatively private.'

It took them seventeen minutes on foot to reach the sea
at the Haven. There was little sand here, just a belt of
shingle curving between two headlands, a naturally private
resort which the lazy or the casual would ignore. Close by
where they came down from the headland a track debouched
on to the beach, leading from the narrow lane which connected with the main road. Outcrops of rock ran out across
the shingle, creating sheltered nooks and private corners.
Further along the beach tiny figures dotted the shingle and
splashed in the water.

There was no doubt that the Haven provided more scope
for staging a drowning than did the main bay. The problem
lay in the timing. Would Tracy have arranged to meet
someone so far from the town, when she had to get back to
work so soon? And if they had met instead in the car park,
would she be persuaded to walk another twenty minutes
further, when it must be plain she would be late back?
Psychologically, too, it was hard to imagine her consenting
to come down to the Haven with a lover she was trying to
shake off. Would she really agree to the idea of a swim in
the nude with someone who had been pestering her? It
hardly seemed likely.

'Good spot for a drowning, sir,' Johnson remarked, bringing Alec back to his original point of departure. He nodded,
and turned back to the path. There seemed little else to be
gained by walking further. As they started to climb, Alec

heard voices below them and looked down to see two teenagers walking past the foot of the path, heading along the
beach.

'Where did those two come from?'

'Sir? Oh, the kids. Along the beach somewhere.'

'No, we could see that way. And they didn't come down
the track from the lane, either. They're going the wrong
way.'

Alec retraced his steps curiously, Johnson following with
more reluctance. Out on the shingle they stumbled and
slipped along until they were under the shadow of the
headland and it seemed they could go no further.

'There's a path under the cliff here. Did you know about
that?'

'Can't say I did, sir. It won't go anywhere.'

'There's only one way to find out. Come on.'

The path was narrow, rising and falling awkwardly as it
wove in and out of the jumbled rocks at the foot of the cliff.
Alec looked up, to see the headland swelling out above their
heads. Soon they were walking through a sort of tunnel,
hollowed out from the soft chalk by the waves. Here and
there, mounds of spoil showed where the cliff had crumbled.

'This must be covered at high water,' Alec said. 'Look at
the seaweed here, and here. What's the tide doing? Any
idea?'

'Couldn't say, sir,' Johnson replied unenthusiastically. 'If
there's any risk of being cut off, shouldn't we go back?' But
Alec was already plunging ahead, eagerly stretching the
muscles which had grown weak and flabby on the beach
and behind the desk.

If the tide had been rising when Tracy was pulled out of
the sea, that must mean it had been pretty well out at the
time she would have been making her way from the pier to
the Haven and back again. What had Farmer said? High
tide about six-thirty; that was Tuesday. Alec snatched a
glance at the hollows and pools. What was the tide doing

now? Angrily, he berated himself because he couldn't remember whether the tides came earlier or later each day.
He glanced again at the line of seaweed. At worst, the top
parts of the path would be no more than a foot or two under
water, but where it dipped the path would be too deep to
stand, and moreover he didn't fancy being battered and
wetted by spray and spindrift for two or three hours. Under
the cliff, where the sun could not penetrate, it was chill and
dank.

They pressed on and miraculously each time the path
seemed to peter out it reappeared just as Alec was thinking
they would have to turn back. Surely now it must go all the
way round? He was almost sure the tide was receding, but
if he was wrong they had gone too far to make it back before
they were cut off. Where the path left the Haven it had been
no more than a few inches above water level. Visions of a
detective-inspector and a detective-constable being rescued
ignominiously from the rocks by the lifeboat flashed through
his mind.

They knew they were round when the tip of the pier, tiny
and ornate, poked round the cliff face. In a few minutes they
rounded a bluff of fallen chalk and there before them was
the bay. The path rose steadily and the sea receded, separated from them by a jumble of rocks. At last, they scrambled
up a chalk slide and found themselves on the tarmac of the
undercliff walk where it terminated in a little sunny garden
with a shelter, and a telescope, and a seat looking out over
the waves. The sun played on the seat invitingly and they
sat down gratefully.

'Twelve minutes to here, sir. It seemed longer.'

'Mm.' Alec looked along to the beach. The tide was going
out. He could see the band of dark sand at its margin.
'Makes it more feasible, doesn't it?' he said. 'Whoever it
was she was meeting could park on the headland and walk
down, and they'd have their little chat walking along the
beach in the Haven. Nice and quiet. She could be out and

back in an hour and a half, if she didn't spend too long with White.'

'She'd ruin her shoes, sir, if she came this way,' Johnson said ruefully, inspecting the sole of one of his stylish trainers.

'She'd take them off. The path's bumpy, but there are no sharp stones. Anyway, maybe she did ruin them. We haven't got them to check.'

'So you think she was killed in the Haven, sir?'

'The beach here—' Alec nodded along towards the pier —'is just too crowded. And how do you get rid of her clothes? But in the Haven, you both leave your clothes on the beach. You go for a swim—and only one of you comes back. He dresses, and bundles things into a bag, and walks away. Nobody's close enough to see any details, or to notice that two of you went into the sea and only one came out.'

'So it comes down to who she could have met.'

'Yes. Checking alibis. The usual dull routine. But it may catch us a murderer, all the same.' He got to his feet, suddenly weary. 'Let's get back,' he said shortly.

CHAPTER 8

It was a quarter to nine by the time Alec had parked his car and was climbing the steps to the club where Martine worked. It had been a wearying journey through the Satur-day evening suburbs, made worse by his own doubts as to whether he should be making the trip at all. Yet, as he knew so well, detection was a matter of using one's contacts as much as using one's brain. Many times in the past he had set out on just such an evening's venture, often with higher stakes—his life, for example—at risk if the evening went wrong. It had been the loneliest variant of a soldier's life in that loneliest of postings.

Now, although the risks were by comparison negligible,

the same keyed alertness, the same simultaneous compulsion and revulsion, gripped him. The evening might bring every-thing—or nothing.

With its venerable exterior and hushed, deeply carpeted hall, the club aped the gentlemen's club of the old sort. The doorman, however, was both too young and too mucular and from behind the inner smoked glass doors oozed the indefinable atmosphere of an institution where only two things are important: the getting, and the losing, of money.

The doorman directed Alec out of the building again and round to an obscure side door in a mews court where an older, seedier version of the same type answered his ring. He found himself in a spartan corridor. Distant murmurs of conversation and the subdued hum of background music could just be heard. The doorman settled back on to his stool, directed a long suspicious look at Alec over the top of his paper, then proceeded to ignore him. It was ten to nine. Alec settled down to wait.

Promptly on the dot of nine the buzz of noise swelled suddenly as a door was opened somewhere out of sight, and Alec bit off a yawn as voices drew nearer and a knot of girls appeared round the corner of the passage. If Martine had not separated herself from the other girls and come over to greet him he would not have known her, so heavily and skilfully were they all made up for the subtly lit world in which they worked. The girls wore the standard hostess's uniform of body-hugging black leotard, black stockings and high heels, with vestigial cream capes across their shoulders, ornamented with the club motif. The impression was imper-sonal, and strangely asexual.

'Hi.' Martine's voice was tired, and the eyes behind the dark lashes fatigued. 'Been waiting long? You should have waited inside. That Herb's a real old woman. He always makes people wait in the corridor.'

'You look as if you've had a hard time.'

'It is hard. You'd better believe it. You let your

concentration slip, and that's the game gone.' She pushed open a door and Alec followed her into the dressing-room. 'Anyone who thinks it's a cushy life wants to try dealing chemmy for an evening. We do half an hour on, half an hour off. Believe me, that's all you can take. This is Fay,' she added, 'and this is Debbie.'

The girls nodded to Alec, one directly, the other in her reflection in the big mirror which ran along one wall. Martine slumped into a chair alongside Debbie and pulled a box of tissues towards her. 'You don't mind waiting while we get out of this lot? Fay's doing us a coffee.'

Alec took a seat. The room was stark, with a minimum of furniture and emulsioned walls; but someone had stuck posters on the walls, and postcards were propped over the mirror. Martine began to smear cold cream on to her face while Fay filled an electric kettle at the basin. Alec took the mug of coffee she handed him, and watched curiously as she joined the other two and they all three dabbed and wiped and peered at their reflections in the mirror. Debbie caught his eye and winked.

'Tagging along with us tonight, I hear?'

'That's right,' Alec said. 'If you'll have me.'

'Depends how you behave.' Her eyes flickered away as she wiped cold cream off, then flickered back, watching him in the mirror. 'Copper. Is that true?'

'That's right.'

'Well, that should put a dampener on the evening, if anything does.'

Martine threw a crumpled tissue in the bin. 'He deserves a night out. He's the one I told you of, who was at Merv's. He's been sorting out Trace's death.'

This time two pairs of eyes shifted sideways in the mirror to watch him. 'Yeah?' said Fay.

'That's right,' said Alec again, and thought wryly that if his contribution to the evening did not become a little more scintillating it would indeed fall flat.

Debbie finished wiping make-up off and gave Alec a speculative look as she went over to the row of pegs by the basin. Alec sipped at his coffee as she kicked off her shoes and began fiddling with the fastening of the ridiculous little cape affair. To divert his thoughts, he asked, 'Do you know where you're going tonight?'

'Out beyond Orpington somewhere. It's a country club. We said we'd meet the others there.'

Out of the corner of his eye, Alec saw Debbie wriggle out of her leotard, and kept his face turned towards Martine's reflection in the mirror. He fancied he descried a glint of amusement in her eyes as they flickered to and fro, and smiled to himself. He had come to find out what he could from these girls, but in their own way he knew they were establishing pretty shrewdly just what sort of a person they were dealing with.

'Don't worry,' Martine said, misconstruing his ex-pression, 'you won't be the only bloke there. Some of the girls'll have a boyfriend along. They'll probably be less keen on you being around, but I expect you can handle that.'

Alec said, 'Is there no boyfriend in your case?'

'That's your job tonight.'

'All right. It'll be a pleasure.'

'That's a comfort. I should hate it to be a trial for you.'

They grinned complicitly in the mirror, and the atmos-phere in the room lightened and settled into what Alec guessed to be its usual after-work tenor. The three girls gossiped and joked, exchanging comments on the clients and the trials of the evening, throwing Alec flashes of explanation whenever he seemed too bemused, and paying him the compliment of treating him as a normal member of their group. Debbie sat back at the mirror in skirt and bra and began to apply make up again, while Fay and Martine went across to change. Alec kept his eyes elsewhere, and they made it easy for him to do so, neither embarrassed nor aggressively provocative in his presence.

Watching them applying final touches of eyeliner and blusher at the mirror, Alec found to his surprise that he was happy to be there. Each was attractive, with the youth, the conventional good looks and full figure which their work required, but there was a good nature in their conversation with each other and their acceptance of himself which he had not anticipated, and he found he was looking forward to the rest of the evening with real pleasure. No wonder Tracy Ashford, brought up in the stuffy, limited life of the south coast town, among the earnest Willie Hendersons and the starchy Sybil Buxteds had found this world so enticing.

Twenty minutes later Alec sat in the front seat of Fay's Mini while she expertly weaved in and out of the traffic on the Vauxhall Bridge Road. From the back, Martine said, 'I hope this evening won't be a waste of time for you. You must be terribly busy trying to find out how she died.'

Alec shrugged and smiled. 'Lots of leads don't get anywhere. I'm only grateful you've given me the chance to come along tonight. And,' he added, 'it's a very pleasant way of spending the evening in any event. If I'm not careful I shall forget about the investigation altogether.'

'Who do you think did it?' Fay asked, with a quick sideways glance.

'Any of half a dozen people we know of so far. There may be many more we know nothing of yet. I suppose what I'm really after tonight is any hint about boyfriends who were too pressing, or contacts she met who might have tried to involve her in anything illegal, or against her will. People who would want to teach her a lesson if she proved uncooperative. Does that sound melodramatic?'

There was a silence, then Martine said, 'I wish it did. You do come across some unpleasant people. If you have any sense you steer clear of them.'

'Unpleasant enough to kill if they were thwarted?'

Martine turned to Debbie. 'Remember Francesca?'

'She killed herself. That was ages ago. Didn't they find

her in her car with a tube connected to the exhaust?'

'Yeah. And we all said how convenient it was for certain people. Remember?'

'For whom?' Alec said. 'What had she been mixed up in?'

Debbie said, 'Drugs. You get asked to help out at a party, only instead of encouraging people to have a glass of champagne you offer them something to smoke, or some pills. She got involved, but then her brother, or cousin, or someone died from drugs and she sort of got converted and wanted out.'

'And the people behind these parties didn't like that?'

'She probably hinted that she'd shop them,' Fay remarked quietly. 'She was quite brave, in her way.'

There was another silence, until Alec said, 'These parties still go on, I suppose?'

'They still go on,' Martine agreed heavily. 'It's not a very clever scene. We steer clear of it. Drugs, protection, big business.'

'But Tracy had time to become involved in it.'

Fay concentrated on scraping between two columns of lorries before the lights changed. As they cleared the junction on amber, she said, 'She was a fool if she did, but none of us knew her well enough to stop her. Only, if you were thinking of asking too many questions tonight about that lot, well, you won't be that popular.'

'It would get back to them that someone was being nosey about their operation?'

Debbie said, 'There's not much that doesn't get back to people like that sooner or later. And it's not so healthy for the girls who have done the talking. And,' she added, 'if you make any official inquiries, well, if you don't mind me saying so, there's a fair amount of "live and let live" among some of your mates.'

'She was drowned, wasn't she?' Fay asked. 'Tracy, I mean.'

'That's right. Made to look as if it might have been an

accident, or suicide—and that's what it'll go down as, if we
don't find a murderer. But she'd been pressed under water
by the looks of it. Her body was naked.'

The three girls were silent as they contemplated the bleak
end of their friend. 'It sounds about their mark,' said Debbie
at last. 'They'd like to make it look like suicide. The naked
bit would just be to make it as nasty as they could for all
her friends and her family and that.'

As the houses and the shopping parades gave way to
garden centres and pony paddocks, Alec asked whether they
recalled any of Tracy's boyfriends pursuing her on one of
these Saturday night outings, and described Guy Ricchi to
them. All three shook their heads.

'It could have been an evening when we were on late shift
and didn't make it,' Martine said. 'Want me to see if I can
jog any memories among the others?'

'I'd like it if you could,' Alec said, and smiled gratefully.

The Mini swung into the drive of the country club, a
rambling, undistinguished Edwardian mansion, carefully
floodlit. The car park suggested a mixed clientele, the odd
Porsche and Mercedes among a selection of sports cars and
souped-up saloons.

'Stick with us,' Martine said, and unexpectedly slipped
her arm through his as they made for the entrance. Alec felt
the warmth of her body and smelt the same clean tang of
soap which he had noted in Mervyn Link's studio, so long
ago it seemed, and his spirits rose. Work and pleasure
usually had to be ruthlessly compartmented in his job, and
it was a relief to find simple ordinariness and good nature
where he had expected hardness and experience. He gave
her arm a squeeze and they followed the others through the
doorway.

Alec was prepared for what they found within. The surface
sophistication, the tiny, crowded square of parquet which
served as a dance floor, the loud music and pretentious
conversations were normally anathema to him, but in this

case the company he found himself in was interesting enough to outweigh his distaste. The group they joined overflowed from a corner where tables had been pushed together. All but a few were girls, linked by the freemasonry of their work: models, croupiers, part-time typists, and in one or two cases, mothers too. With them were three or four men, favoured escorts treated with tolerance or disdain, conscious of being present on sufferance. A youthful banker gazed around in disbelief, while an older man watched his companion, a dazzling black girl, with proprietorial arrogance that Alec could see was not looked on too kindly. He wondered what they made of him, and how many of them knew who he was and why he was there.

He danced with most of the girls, and with Martine several times, and the time passed pleasantly enough, if not very fruitfully. After a while, though, Martine disappeared in the direction of the Ladies' and when she returned she tapped him on the shoulder and gestured him to follow her. In the front lobby, where there was a bar and the music was more restrained, sat the black dancer at a small table.

'This is Ginetta,' Martine said, making the introductions. 'She remembers Tracy's doctor friend.'

Alec bought them drinks, and they sat at the table. In a voice of second-generation cockney at curious odds with her aristocratic features, Ginetta replied to Alec's questions calmly enough. It was soon plain that the man she remembered was indeed Guy Ricchi.

'He came to the flat, a year or so back, with Tracy.'

'As long ago as that?' Alec asked. 'I don't suppose he came again later?'

'Sure he did, but without Trace. Back in the spring, I guess.'

'To see you?'

Ginetta's eyes flashed with amusement. 'Not his type, man. He was looking for Tracy, and Tracy was out with the girls.'

'And you weren't?'

'I was otherwise engaged,' she said with heavy irony. 'Tracy's boy came in the middle of that . . . engagement.'

'I don't suppose he was very popular with you for that. He just wanted to know where she was?'

'Man, he was so wound up I thought he was going to snap. He banged the door so loud, and so long, we had to let him in.'

'And did you tell him where Tracy was?'

She shook her head. 'No way. He was going to be bad news for somebody, and when they're in that mood you just keep them out of the way. They find someone else, they get over it.'

'He didn't threaten you?'

'Sure he threatened me. But I had a friend with me who don't like to be threatened. He was keeping out of things, on account of he was still trying to find his trousers, but when he hears this boy trying to put the arm on he came and persuaded him to be more polite.'

Alec smiled. 'I think I get the picture. What I'm wondering is whether he found Tracy, and whether he was violent to her when he did.'

'She don't have no marks on her when I see her next. That sort of boy,' she said dismissively, 'they don't hit you. Too well brought up. Sure he found her. She told him to get lost. She said.'

'You asked her?'

'The girl shrugged. 'She told me anyway. Apology for him having disturbed me. That's the last I hear of him.'

Alec smiled gratefully. 'Thanks. Forget I asked so many questions. No point in spoiling your evening.'

'You're welcome. You ain't so bad. For a copper,' she added with a malicious smile.

'Thanks.'

She turned to Martine, who had been sitting a little apart, reluctant to intrude. 'You going with this one?' she asked, and without waiting for an answer, went on, 'You watch him. He's nice. But if you're not careful, you going to get involved. An' then you'll find him mighty dangerous.'

'Sorry about that,' Martine said as they took their drinks back into the main room. 'They're all dying to know whether I brought you because . . . you know.'

'I know,' Alec said, 'and it was brave of you to do it. Knowing that they're bound to be wondering.'

She glanced at him sideways, and he thought she looked tired suddenly. After all, it had been a long evening for her. 'Yeah,' she said, 'I guess I'll just have to put up with that.'

They joined the rest of the group, squeezing in round the tiny, awkward tables with difficulty. By now it was common knowledge that Alec was a policeman, but Martine skilfully implied that he was there as her escort, rather than by way of duty. As the evening wore on, however, and talk became freer, Tracy Ashford's death came to be the subject that occupied them all, and a general discussion developed, with theories flying to and fro, earnestly put forward and as earnestly scorned. Alec took as little part as he could, trusting to the general flow to throw up possibilities he might not have thought of. After all, these people had known the dead girl in the last months of her life, and understood better than any what sort of life it had been.

The fact that Tracy had been burdened by an unwelcome lover was common knowledge, and majority opinion cast him as the villain. It was a commonplace to these girls that ditched lovers had a habit of turning awkward, and the most testing part of their handling of any affair was its ending. The banker looked more thoughtful.

'There's always the few that turn really nasty,' Debbie said calmly. 'He's got to be your top suspect.' Alec wondered what they would say if he told them that Ricchi had disappeared the day after Tracy's murder.

One girl said, 'I still think the most likely thing is some game that went wrong. You know, you get to larking about and if you're not careful you try something a bit too risky and it goes wrong. After all, it's pretty ace, doing it in the sea. Maybe she was with some guy that just couldn't stop.'

It was a possibility which Alec had considered carefully, and he had gone so far as to ring the pathologist to discuss it. The upshot was that the injuries before death were not inconsistent, but it was less likely that the post-mortem injuries could have been obtained in this way and there were no definite signs of intercourse. Alec had filed this solution as possible, but unlikely.

'The boyfriend done it,' Debbie repeated decisively. 'After all, who else could've? There wasn't anyone else we knew that was that crazy about her. I mean, Merv hardly fits the bill.' There was a general buzz of laughter, and Martine leant over to whisper a word in Alec's ear. It certainly sounded as if Link was unlikely to have formed any attachment of a passionate nature for Tracy.

'There's others than Merv,' another girl said. Alec glanced at her. Heavily painted, coarser featured than the others, she seemed also more aggressive and cynical. 'What about Kerim? What about his parties?' The harsh voice went on insistently in the sudden quiet. 'Little Tracy Ashford, the innocent from the country. It didn't take her long to join the grown-ups, did it? If you want to find a killer, you'll find plenty to choose from among Kerim's outfit.'

Alec looked round the faces of the girls, sobered, evasive and even, he realized with interest, frightened. None of them wanted to continue with this subject, but none had the strength to speak up and bring it to an end. His gaze passed from face to face, to rest again on that of the girl who had spoken. Her eyes met his, hard, and old, and he looked steadily back. Her stare dropped, and she muttered something.

There was an uncomfortable hiatus, broken determinedly by Ginetta. 'Come on, lover boy,' she said, and got to her feet, pulling her escort after her with more gentleness than she had shown him that evening. 'Time for a last dance.'

The group broke up, deciding in unspoken consent that it was time to go, looking for a last drink, a final dance. Alec and Martine shuffled on to the diminutive dance floor and jigged aimlessly together until Alec caught sight of the girl's anxious, unhappy expression and forced himself to smile and divert her thoughts. It was the least he could do in return for an evening which, he suspected, she would look back on with little pleasure.

Later, they sat crushed together in Fay's Mini. The car was overfull and Martine sat on Alec's knee in the back, delicately holding herself a little apart from him to show that whatever assumptions the other girls made, she knew he was there from duty. Alec shifted his weight until he could put an arm around her and draw her head down on to his shoulder, and reflected that it was a good thing he had brought his own car into town.

The Mini dropped them by the club, and they walked silently the few streets to where he had parked. 'Thanks for all your help,' Alec said as they drove towards her flat. 'You didn't have to do it, and I'm grateful.'

'Somebody has to.' She shivered, though the night was warm. 'I hope someone does as much for me, when it's my turn.'

Alec glanced at her sharply, and said nothing. A little later, she said, 'Sorry. It's difficult to be very cheerful about it. I hope you didn't find the evening too boring,' she added formally.

They drew up outside the grim block where Martine shared a flat. 'No,' Alec said gently. 'It wasn't boring.'

'I'm glad. I'm glad it was useful.'

'It was more than just useful. I enjoyed being with you. It was kind of you to give me the opportunity.'

She sighed. 'We're not so very awful, are we?' Alec turned to her, but she hurried on. 'I suppose you're going to say you've got to get back now. It's no use me asking you to come in for a cup of coffee?'

'No, it's no use. It wouldn't be, would it?'

Martine looked straight ahead, out of the windscreen, at the parked cars and the street lamps. 'Be thankful for small mercies,' she said in a small voice. Then she turned to him, and managed a smile, and held out her hand. Alec took it, and gave it a squeeze, and smiled back.

'See you. Thanks for the lift.'

She got out of the car and climbed the stairs to the heavy front door. She took the key from her bag without looking back, turned the lock and went in. Alec sighed, and started the car. As he drove away through the empty streets towards the road south he tried to turn his mind to considering what he had learnt from the evening. But he kept hearing again Martine's voice as she reminded herself to be thankful for small mercies, and the smell of her cleanliness lingered in the car, and he wished that the price that had to be paid for the evening's progress did not have to be paid by her.

CHAPTER 9

'Kerim Halfaya,' Alec said, as he and the Superintendent sat in Alec's office later that Sunday morning. 'It has to be the same. I got Johnson on to tracing Link's business partner, with an eye to finding out something about these parties that Link supplied girls for. Well, that business partner is a company wholly owned by one Kerim Halfaya. Libyan passport, been in this country six years. Described as businessman, which covers a multitude of sins. Remember when a policewoman was shot at the Libyan Embassy? Halfaya was one of the characters we found inside. Just enough diplomatic immunity to avoid paying his parking fines, but on the other hand is involved in trade deals which are thought to be generally profitable to us. As to the parties, the Met have raided two, and found nothing more sinful than a group of businessmen having a quiet drink with a bunch of good-looking girls. They've a good idea there's more to them than that, but can't justify poking their noses in again for a while.'

'Humph.' The Super looked at Alec shrewdly. 'You didn't find all that out just by getting Johnson to ask a few questions.' Alec kept his face carefully expressionless. During his time in Army intelligence he had made a number of contacts with opposite numbers in the various security forces, and from time to time he felt it was wise to check that these channels were still open. He knew that the Super guessed that that was where the information on Halfaya had come from—and guessed, too, that sometime in the future the favour would be repaid.

'It gets us nowhere,' the Super said. 'Not as it stands. So the girl went to the odd party now and again. You might just as well suspect the baker because she went to him to buy bread.'

'There is the girl Francesca that they mentioned, sir.'

'What about her?'

'Well, on the face of it that was another death which could have been staged—probably was, if you believe the people I spoke with last night. The inquest verdict was apparently "suicide while the balance of the mind was disturbed", but it was a highly convenient death, and again Kerim is the one who is implicated.'

The Super shook his head. 'It's too thin, Alec. If you want me to buy it you'll have to find something more substantial. And if Halfaya is the master criminal you think he is, everyone will be frightened of what might happen if word gets back to him that they've been gossipping.'

'I think they are, sir. I'll be lucky if I find someone who knows anything and is willing to talk.'

'But you'll try. They'll be doing everyone a favour if they give us something hard against this bloke.'

'Maybe. Don't people like him always wriggle clear? That's why people won't talk. They know he's never going to end up behind bars.'

'You'll have to do what you can, all the same, Alec. Right, what about Ricchi? Where is he?'

'I've had Detective-Sergeant Pringle up there checking it out, sir. There's little enough to add. He hasn't taken much with him, and more important, he hasn't cleaned out his bank and building society accounts. His partners aren't very pleased with him, of course, but it seems he did have some time off due to him. Our best lead is the car, which could be anywhere. We're checking the long-term car parks at the airports and so on, of course. I've told Pringle to come back. The routine work he can do as easily from here, and a lot more cheaply.'

'Good. Now, this chap Richardson. The councillor. You say he's been spinning you a line?'

Alec nodded. 'He said he'd never met Tracy except at the occasional social do. But he'd taken her out on a one to one basis at least once.'

'Dirty old man, is he?'

'Yes, I think he is,' Alec said feelingly. 'He has a strong line in the bluff businessman act, but my own view is that he has only one priority in his life, and that's Councillor Richardson.'

'Want to have another go at him? While I'm around?'

'Love to, sir, if you can spare the time.'

'Good. Get hold of him, and we'll go directly.'

'I've got you another recruit,' the Super said with a sideways glance as they sat in the car park of Richardson Plastics. 'Only one, I'm afraid. The best I can do.'

'Thank you, sir. Even one'll help.'

Despite it being a Sunday, Richardson had insisted on

meeting at the factory, and Alec had been prepared to humour him on that point. But he was regretting it now. Richardson would enjoy keeping them waiting. He looked out at the car park and the swell of the downs beyond and to fill in the time told the other man what they had found out about Mr Richardson of Richardson Plastics. There was little that was concrete: speeding tickets, parking. A hint of ambiguity over election expenses when he first got on to the council. The building of the industrial estate where they were parked had caused more controversy. It had been green belt land, with a collection of run-down farm buildings and a dilapidated farmhouse. The house and buildings had been flattened in a day, one bank holiday, and by coincidence the notice scheduling them as listed buildings had arrived the following day. The council decided that, with the buildings gone, the site was spoilt anyway and gave permission for development of the estate.

'And Richardson owned the land, of course?' the Super asked.

'That's right.'

A large Mercedes drifted into the car park and drew up against the factory wall. The two policemen climbed out of their car and made their way over to meet Richardson, the Superintendent introducing himself briefly. Richardson fished for a key with an affable, slightly puzzled expression and led the way through the echoing office to his own room. 'I hoped we'd mentioned everything last time this young man called. Not that I'm unwilling to help in any way I can. Are you finding difficulty clearing up the poor girl's death?'

'We're having some trouble,' the Superintendent said bluntly, 'with people telling us less than the truth.'

Richardson, who had been settling himself proprietorially behind his desk, stiffened. 'Oh yes?'

'One of them being yourself, Councillor Richardson. You told Detective-Inspector Stainton here that you hadn't met

Tracy Ashford except at one or two social functions where
she appeared as Miss Southern Belle.'

'Well, I don't know exactly what my words . . .'

'You didn't say you'd taken her out to dinner, just the
two of you, did you? See what I mean about telling less
than the truth? Like to make amends now, if you please,
Councillor?'

Richardson's amiable smile had hardened and his eyes
were cold as he considered the other man's words.

'All right,' the Superintendent said. 'What about this one?
On the day Tracy drowned, we know you were out of the
office between twelve and three-thirty. That's a simple
matter of checking facts. Care to enlighten us about your
whereabouts between those times?'

'Who've you been talking to?' Richardson said, and his
eyes narrowed as he looked from the Superintendent to Alec
and back again.

'Never you mind,' the Super said. 'Suppose you give us
some answers, Mr Richardson. We'll cope with the questions. You took Tracy Ashford out for dinner before you
took her title away from her, didn't you? True or false?'

'All right, true. To explain that there was no personal
animosity. So that she would know we were acting in the
best interests of the town, and in her best interests, too.'

'And was it in the best interests of the town for you to
take her up on to the downs afterwards? Was it decided in
a council meeting that you should have it off with her, just
to show there was no personal animosity?'

'Now you look here . . .' Richardson began, and the
veneer of amiability had vanished completely.

'No, you look here. That trip to the downs is a fact. Now,
I'm a simple policeman and I like facts. I want some
more of them. So sharpen up your memory, Councillor
Richardson. I don't want it playing any little tricks on you.
Facts. All right?'

'All right. The fact is that Tracy Ashford was a little tart

who sold her fanny about every photographer's studio in
the south, and if I took her up on to the downs you can bet
your life it wasn't the first time she'd seen them by moon-
light, not by a long chalk.'

'Where did you give her dinner?'

'We drove out.' He gave the name of a steakhouse.

'That was the going rate, was it? One steak, medium rare,
in return for a piece of the action?'

'She was a slut who'd do it for nothing. I treated her too
well, if you want to know.'

'And how did she treat you? Did she give you your
reward?'

'That's my business.'

'Happened before, had it?'

'Not with me. But ask anyone what she was like. She was
asking for it. A cheap tart.'

'Try telling us the truth about that evening, Mr Richardson. Whether she was a tart or not I don't know. I never
met her. But she didn't oblige you that night, did she? Steak
and ice-cream didn't get Tracy Ashford into the back seat
for you, did it? Well?'

'All right. As it happens, it didn't. Probably just as well.
I don't want to catch anything.'

Alec clenched his teeth, but the Super ground remorselessly on. 'Humiliating, was it? This teenager telling you
where to get off? Resentful, were you?'

'Not resentful enough to kill her, you'd better believe me.'

'But resentful enough to make sure she had her title taken
away.'

'She brought that on herself. Everyone knows. Showing
her tits off in the papers like the tart she was.'

'But the papers hadn't appeared when the decision was
taken.'

Richardson's eyes narrowed. 'If you want to know, she'd
been doing photos like that for months. In magazines.'

'But you did fix for her to have her title taken away?'

'No comment.'

'And have you no comment on where you were last Tuesday, when you were out of the office for almost four hours in the middle of the day?'

Alec watched the pallor of the businessman's skin, and how his breath came in starts, and wondered about the state of his heart.

'I often have to be away from the factory. I'd have to check my diary. Or I could have been at home and gone on to a meeting after lunch.'

'At home with your wife. And does she know of the interest you took in the welfare of a little tart? Used to it, is she?'

Red spots appeared on Richardson's cheeks. Casually, the Super leant forward and pulled a desk diary out of a tray and began to leaf through the pages.

'One o'clock, lunch at home,' the Super quoted slowly. 'And underneath, where it says "HCP, TA": care to explain that?'

'Heathcote Plastics. We do thousands of pounds' worth of business with them. There's nothing in that. TA just means "telephone appointment".'

'Not "Tracy Ashford"? Not "headland car park"? Who made the appointment—you or her?'

'I was at home. Ask my wife.'

'We will.'

'So you see that I have an alibi, Superintendent. What a disappointment for you. I'm not a murderer after all.'

And he looked at the two policemen with a slow, sarcastic smile spreading over his features, knowing they could only check, and cross check, and hope for something fresh to come to light. Alec's heart sank, for with a man as devious and as clever as Richardson—clever enough to leave his diary intact, to arrange fall-back after fall-back in explanation—there would be no short cuts, and possibly no success at the end of the day. They left soon afterwards, Richardson's words echoing tauntingly in their ears.

'It's going to be a hard case to bring off, Alec,' the Super said eventually as they wove back through the suburbs towards the town centre. 'If it was Richardson, and he killed her down at the Haven, we're looking for the lucky break, the chance sighting, the sort of thing that comes out of a thousand questions—if you're lucky. But there are too many other possibilities. Assuming she ever left the pier, we don't know Tracy reached the headland, or the Haven. She could have met one of Halfaya's henchmen, looking to settle his score, or Ricchi, or Henderson.'

'And which of them, if any, was it that she had planned to see?' Alec asked. 'Which of them was it she dressed for? Because if she was out to taunt any of them, she was playing a dangerous game. Henderson with his flaming temper? Richardson? Ricchi, obsessed with the ending of their relationship?'

'She spent too much time playing dangerous games,' the Super said abruptly. 'That's the trouble with girls like her. They don't realize that to the man it may not be a game at all. Until they find themselves raped, or dead.'

Jayne Simmonds came out of the railway station into the sun of the forecourt and looked about her. The eyes of the drivers of the station taxis turned towards her from the shadow of their cars where they whiled away the day, sizing her up where she stood, not fidgeting, but self-possessed, orientating herself perhaps from a map carried in her mind. A small suitcase was in her hand, a tapestry bag over the other shoulder. Perhaps it was the meagreness of her luggage, or perhaps something in her demeanour which made the taxi-drivers mutter to themselves, 'Business, not pleasure.' They watched warily as she began to walk towards them, and the driver of the car at the front of the rank folded his paper and made to lean across to the passenger door; but she kept going with a fleeting apologetic smile, past the taxis and across the road, heading towards the sea.

The day was hot, and she walked further than many might have chosen to, encumbered as she was, past the cafés and arcades, past the newsagents and the shoe shops, and into the square where the town hall and a chain store faced the police station and the Methodist church in the afternoon sun. She glanced towards the police station and her pace faltered, then she continued on out of the square towards the front, unhurried, unflustered in the heat.

At the promenade Jayne turned left and followed the road towards the distant cliffs, counting off the side roads until she turned left again up a narrow, car-lined street and into a small square, where she climbed the steps into the shade of the Logan Hotel.

Miss Helston was behind the reception desk. In a wicker chair, the Captain snored away the heat of the day. A labrador snoozed in the shade under one of the tables, looking at her under its lids and half pricking one ear.

'My name is Simmonds,' Jayne said quietly. 'I don't know whether it was you I spoke to on the telephone?'

'It was,' Miss Helston said, glancing at the Captain's slumped form. 'Everything is quite in order. I expect you'd like to see the room and have a chance to recover from your journey.'

'That's very kind of you.'

'We'll be serving tea before very long. Would you like me to give you a call? Or shall I bring you a pot up?'

Jayne smiled, and shook her head: 'I'll come down for it. I'm putting you to a lot of trouble as it is.'

'No trouble,' Miss Helston beamed. 'But if you come down you must expect the residents to be rather interested in you.' She lowered her voice. 'They're a nice bunch, but we're all a little eccentric here,' and she nodded towards the Captain affectionately.

'Come far?' Miss Wynne-Andrews asked penetratingly.

'Not far.'

'Which room have they given you? Hey?'

'It's at the top. Facing towards the sea.'

'Humph. "Facing towards" is all right. But can you see it?'

'You can,' Jayne said, amused. 'If you try a little.'

Miss Wynne-Andrews nodded, acknowledging Jayne's answer, content in her own occupation of the hotel's best room. 'It's all right,' she consented, 'but they're a pair of old fuddy-duddies. I always expect,' she continued remorselessly, not troubling to lower her voice, 'to see that dog of theirs round 'em up one day like a pair of sheep.'

Jayne caught Miss Helston's eye across the foyer and was rewarded with a solemn wink. She smiled, and turned back to Miss Wynne-Andrews.

'And then, would you believe, last week one of the guests was arrested on the steps of the hotel. Ar—rest—ed.'

'Indeed?'

'I assure you. And that same afternoon a young woman, yes, a young woman, was pulled out of the sea quite dead. And quite naked.' She paused. 'The Captain suggests that the events are linked. I reserve judgment.'

Not half you don't, Jayne thought to herself. Aloud, she said, 'What became of him? The young man, I mean?'

'As he was here again the following day, I can only imagine that he is not, at present, thought to be a murderer. It puts one in an unpleasant position, Miss . . .'

'Simmonds,' said Jayne.

'. . . Miss Simmonds. One has to pass in the corridor. One has to say good morning. It is very awkward.'

'I'm sure it must be.' There was a snort from behind them and Jayne turned to see the Captain staring angrily across the foyer towards the entrance. Jayne followed his gaze. At the top of the steps stood Alec, one hand still holding the door open, and for a moment Jayne watched him unnoticed, and thought how gaunt he looked. Beneath the tan there were dark smudges around his eyes. Hesitantly, she rose and walked towards him.

'Hello, Alec,' she said. She watched his gaze shift to her, saw what she hadn't expected, nervousness at her sudden appearance, heard that same nervousness in his voice, making it abrupt.

'What are you doing here?'

'The Super asked me to come, to lend a hand. If you'll let me.'

'Well, he never asked me,' Alec said. He looked around at the veiled eagerness of the faces sipping tea, and grimaced, then went across to Miss Helston and murmured something in her ear. She smiled and nodded, and Jayne heard her say, 'Only for half an hour, mind.'

'That's all right,' Alec said, returning. 'Tea'll wait for us if we're not too long. Come on.'

Together, they strolled down on to the promenade, crossed the road and leant against the railings. Beneath them on the beach, children played and adults dozed. Distant splashings in the shallows were accompanied by shrieks and shouts which wafted across the sands on the zephyrs of the famed ozone.

'The Super asked you to come?' Alec regretted his earlier curtness, and tried to make his voice more welcoming.

'He asked me if I'd like to,' Jayne said soberly. 'I'm not sure it wasn't one of the most uncharacteristic things I've known. I've always assumed he rather had it in for me, if he even knew who I was. But yesterday I got a call when I went back to the station, and there he was at the other end. Just his normal self in most respects—rude, you know, and hoping to rile—but he said you'd been assigned to a suspicious death which might or might not be murder, and if you wanted me . . . if you wanted my help,' she corrected herself, 'he thought it would be a good idea if I lent a hand. I was supposed to be doing schools visits all this week, but he just said to cancel them and come on down.' She glanced at him. 'I was certainly rather surprised you didn't know I was coming.' She kept the most surprising piece of information to herself. Why, after all, should the Super have recommended the Logan Hotel?

'He told me someone was coming, but not who,' Alec said bitterly. 'His little joke.'

They were silent a moment. On the beach, a toddler intently pulled the tail of a sleeping puppy. The puppy finally snapped and the child began to cry in a bored manner.

'Do you want me to stay?' she asked quietly.

Alec hesitated, knowing that she had to, and that much as the Super might enjoy toying with them, he had assigned her to the case in lucid appreciation of the manpower requirements Alec faced. Sending her back was not an option, even if Alec could have borne to do it. To have her here would be a constant trial. Nevertheless, he could not find it in him to wish they could be parted.

'Let me tell you something about the case,' he said at last. They gazed out at the fringe of green on the horizon, where a cross-Channel ferry winked in the sunlight, and he told her what they knew, and as he did so he thought of the pallid figure in the mortuary drawer, and of the cheeky grin of the girl who looked out from the back of the office door, and Jayne heard with concern the note of tiredness and something more, bitterness, in his voice and wished things had worked out differently between them.

'Pringle should be back this afternoon,' he finished. 'There's another WPC here, too, a nice kid. You'll like her.'

He turned and looked at her, and she read the unspoken question in his eyes.

'I'm glad I can be some use,' she said. 'But, Alec, nothing else has changed. I'm sorry.'

'No. Of course.' He turned away.

'I've a room in the Logan Hotel. Would you like me to move? I easily can.'

'Good Lord, no.' He grinned, and they both relaxed. 'It's

an education in itself to stay in that place, and in any event you won't get better looked after anywhere on the south coast. Have they told you yet about me being hauled off to gaol in the dead of night?'

'I did hear something,' she smiled.

Alec chuckled. 'I felt I'd made a contribution of a modest sort to their enjoyment. But don't underestimate the residents of that place. Their intelligence network is every bit as efficient as any I've ever come across. Anyway, we have some interesting encounters on the stairway, I assure you.'

'It's a shame your holiday has to be spoilt, sir, all the same.'

'Mm. That reminds me . . .' Alec's voice tailed off, and he looked along to his left among the brightly coloured windbreaks. Jayne watched him covertly and guessed what he was about to say.

'Look,' he said, still turned away from her, 'I'm not going to make it back to the hotel for tea.'

'All right, sir.' Jayne made her tone bright and helpful. 'I'll pop along to the station afterwards, shall I?'

'Yes, why don't you. But we'll try and make it back to the Logan for dinner.'

Jayne turned away, crossing the wide pavement and the busy road. At the corner she looked back. Alec was gone, and hunting along the front she saw his spare figure marching briskly along and suddenly dive down the stairs to the beach. So that was how it was. She sighed, and turned back towards the hotel, and tea.

CHAPTER 10

The atmosphere in the cramped police station was not easy that Sunday evening. Detective-Sergeant Pringle, returned from his fruitless trip to the Midlands, was in sullen mood.

Liz Pink, who had had a tiff with her boyfriend over her unavailability to join him that day, was engaged in the laborious work of checking traffic reports and routine patrol records in the hope that somewhere there would be a note of Councillor Richardson's car being seen in the vicinity of the headland on the day of Tracy's death. Earlier, Liz had endured a futile interview with an obviously scared and dominated Mrs Richardson who had confirmed every word of her husband's alibi over that fateful lunch time. Jayne joined Andy Johnson in the search for any trace of the missing Dr Guy Ricchi. Ensconced in his sultry office, Alec puzzled over the possibilities, re-read the post-mortem report a dozen times and tried to work out a strategy for approaching the shadowy Kerim.

As is the way of things, they worked all through that evening with no reward, but no sooner had Liz Pink resumed her task on Monday morning that she had a breakthrough. It was not, however, Alec thought as he stared at the brief note, a very helpful one. The last thing he needed at the moment was for the circle of suspects to be widened.

He called in John Pringle and handed him the sheet of paper.

'Have a look at that list of traffic offences.'

Pringle read it briefly. 'Bloody fool,' he said. 'Why on earth couldn't he have said so?'

Alec shrugged. 'He's certainly not a practised criminal, anyhow, if he thought we'd miss it. You'd better bring him in, John. Don't be too gentle—if you take a hardish line with him, I'll play the understanding older brother once we've got him in the interview room.'

'Think he did it? I wouldn't have thought he'd have the nerve.'

'Nor would I. It'll save us a lot of work if he did.'

An hour and a half later Alec faced Willie Henderson across the table in the bare interview room, while Liz Pink sat by the door, notebook at the ready. The boy seemed to have shrunk, and the too-sharp suit hung upon him like poor fancy dress.

'You'd have done better to own up straight away,' Alec said sadly. 'Now tell us exactly what your movements were that day. WPC Pink is going to write it all down, and we'll have it drawn up in the form of a statement for you to sign. We've no time for games. Do Tracy the favour of telling us the truth.'

Liz Pink smiled encouragingly at the boy, and held her pencil poised. Slowly, in fits and starts, the story emerged. Henderson had seen Tracy on the Sunday afternoon before her death. The night before, it seemed, she had been in London.

'The thing is, she hated those parties,' Henderson said bitterly, 'I know she did. So why go to them?'

'How many had she been to?'

'I don't know. Three, maybe. Four.'

'Do you know what went on there?'

He shook his head, and Alec wondered how much he had guessed at, or how much he had tortured himself with wild speculation. 'So how do you know she hated them?'

'You could tell, that's all.' He shrugged. 'Little things. And if you asked, she'd change the subject. She was sort of subdued.'

Not, Alec agreed, her normal condition. Henderson had been to the house on Sunday afternoon, to see if Tracy would come out for a walk or a drive with him. She had been listless and disinclined to make any effort. He had tried to rouse her, and to comfort her, putting an arm round her, but she had shaken him off and told him she preferred him not to touch her. Henderson had made some remark about his concern for her and she had told him, rudely, that she didn't want his concern. Alec, reading between the lines, saw the harshness of her rebuke and the hopelessness of Henderson's love for her.

He hadn't stayed more than half an hour on the Sunday, but his concern for her, he said, persisted, and in his lonely driving to and from appointments on Monday he had explored his aching care for her over and over again. By Tuesday morning he had convinced himself that the only way out, and the only way to help her, was to see her again and tell her directly that she had to change her way of life because her friends could not bear to stand by while she did herself such harm. Alec felt for Henderson's passion and his inexperience, remembering enough from his own youth to know how such passion could eat its way into its host.

The upshot was, according to Henderson, that he wangled his appointments to give him just time to drive to the coast and see Tracy as she left work at lunch-time. If he could do that, he had reasoned, and could keep himself calm, he might at least show himself a concerned friend, and maybe persuade her to spend the evening with him, re-establishing their old trust and comradeship. It was the naïve, impetuous plan of an adolescent. According to Henderson, he had cut his last client short in the morning and driven straight to the health centre, only to find that Tracy had already left.

'I knew then that it was probably a mistake,' he muttered. 'But I had to go on, having started, like.'

He had therefore driven slowly down into the town, doing his best to scan the busy pavements while negotiating the narrow streets. When he got down to the seafront he had found a parking place with difficulty, a long way along the promenade. Then he had started back on foot, in his foolish and doomed endeavour to find one girl in all the crowds.

Of course he had failed, he said. He had gone on looking, walking the alleys and sidestreets, to and fro along the front, missing lunch, hot and uncomfortable in his collar and tie. Finally, defeated, he had made his way back to the car. Even then he had searched the pavements as he drove up through the town until, with hope finally expired, the shops left behind and the suburbs opening out, he had pressed the accelerator harder to the floor and been pulled in by the routine traffic patrol which lay in wait for over-exuberant tourists. The result was a ticket, and an even more irate client waiting for him at his next appointment.

'So you never did get to see Tracy that day.'

'No.'

Alec regarded the boy speculatively. 'When did you hear she was dead?'

Henderson stared miserably at his feet. 'It was on the local radio that afternoon. At first, just that a girl had been drowned. The next bulletin said that it was Tracy.'

'It must have hurt,' Alec murmured sympathetically.

'It was all those people looking at her,' Henderson burst out. 'Because she wasn't wearing anything. That's what I couldn't bear. They weren't interested in her, they didn't care whether she was alive or dead.' Angry tears brimmed in his eyes and he brushed at them roughly. 'They didn't care, she wasn't a person to them. It was just her nakedness they wanted. To gloat over.'

That was it, Alec knew. Strangers, uncaring, ignorant, had pawed Tracy's body with their eyes, on the beach, in the magazines and pin-ups, while setting no value on the person within, which Henderson had loved so dearly. Or had he? Had it really been the contrast between their lust and his love, or the fact that he had known no more of her than anyone might which had been impossible to bear? Had he been in love not with the person, not even with the laughing, pouting face, but with the breasts, the thighs, the secret, inaccessible parts? Sexual jealousy. Jagged. Unremitting. Its force unworn by the years. Murderous.

Alec got to his feet and wandered over to the window. Below in the courtyard, two shirtsleeved policemen leant against a patrol car and their laughter drifted up to him. 'Can anyone corroborate this?' he asked, turning back to the boy.

'They know I called at the house on Sunday. The nurse

at the health centre will remember, too. It was her that told
me Tracy had gone for her lunch.'

'And after that,' Alec said gently. 'On the front. It's pay
and display, isn't it? Did you keep the ticket? Did you see
anyone you knew, anyone at all?'

Henderson shook his head. Alec asked him to wait while
the notes were typed up, a forlorn, very young figure.

'It's not very hopeful for him, is it, sir?' Liz said when
they had left the boy to his own thoughts with a uniformed
constable to watch over him.

'It's useless as an alibi,' Alec sighed. 'That's about its
only redeeming feature. Other than that, he had every
opportunity to meet the girl and kill her. The only thing is,
did she know he was coming or not? If he's telling the truth,
and she didn't, then there was still someone else she was
planning to meet—the person she dressed for so specially.
We'll check what we can, of course.'

Liz grimaced. 'It seems all wrong that that sort of infatuation could lead to murder. He's only a child. Everybody
gets things out of proportion when they're young.' Alec
glanced at her, amused, and she smiled. 'I know. I'm talking
like an experienced old woman. I'll go and get these notes
sorted out.'

Later, when they had let Henderson go, Alec sat at his
desk with the statement in front of him. Dawn, Tracy's
housemate, had confirmed Henderson's visit to the house
on the Sunday, and the practice nurse remembered his
calling at the health centre. Alec was relieved that the boy's
story had not been instantly demolished, although it left the
conundrum unsolved. Henderson, Ricchi, Richardson. All
pursuing one nineteen-year-old would-be model. Which of
them had met her that Tuesday lunch-time for a last, fateful
swim?

Jayne stayed in the car while Alec climbed the steps and
spoke into the entryphone of the flat. Inside, Martine met

him at the head of the stairs, and ushered him into the flat
without a word. He saw the apprehension, and the carefully
suppressed hope, in her eyes. She seemed smaller, and more
ordinary, and he knew it was because he had robbed her of
her self-confidence.

He made no attempt to pretend. 'I've come with more
questions about Tracy Ashford's death. I'm sorry, Martine.'
He held her gaze while the hope drained away, then she
shrugged and turned to fiddle with an ornament on the
mantel.

'What do you want?' she said evenly.

'I've got to know more about Kerim.'

'Of course. I was a fool, that day at Merv's, wasn't I?'

'Tracy may have come to the same end that Francesca
did. I want to talk to someone who went to those parties.'

'And then? Will you leave me alone?'

'If you like. I wish we could have met in different circumstances.'

'Oh yeah, if you weren't a copper, and I was a nice girl,'
she said with bitter emphasis.

'Look,' Alec said, 'we've only met twice. It's not part of
my plan to involve you. If it makes any difference, I wish
you hadn't spoken to me at Merv's, too, if it makes things
difficult for you. But that's past regretting now.' He watched
her trying hard not to hate him, ungainly and vulnerable.
'When this is over,' he said on impulse, '—and it will
be, in due course—and I'm not a copper working on a case
any more, I'd like, I really would like, to take you out
one evening. For a meal, or a show, maybe. Could we do
that?'

'Sure we could do that. I don't know any better, do I?
And you'd be kind and thoughtful, and say thank you for
my help, and perhaps to show you were really human you'd
stay the night. We'd have a lovely time, right?'

She turned, and Alec looked at her soberly. 'Sorry,' she
said with a wan smile. 'It's the novelty. You get too used to

the men who are just out for all they can get. I never asked you. Are you married? Kids?'

'No. Not married. No kids.'

'Right,' she said more briskly. 'You want to have a little chat with Sandra. You'll remember Sandra when you meet her. I'll give her a ring and you can go and see her. You won't mind if I don't come with you.' Quickly, efficiently, she moved to the phone and made the arrangements, then wrote the address on a piece of paper for Alec and followed him to the door.

'Look,' he began, 'it's nothing to do with . . .' but she interrupted him brightly, wishing him luck.

'Nice to see you again,' she said. Alec sighed, and started down the stairs.

It took them fifteen minutes of weary weaving in and out of car-lined streets to find Sandra's flat. He knew her as soon as she opened the door to them: the cynical, worldly-wise girl who had been the only one to talk openly of Kerim and his drug-pushing parties two nights before. She stood aside for them to enter, and watched them warily as they found a seat.

'How're you going to keep my name out of this?' she asked bluntly. 'How're you going to protect me?'

'I can't give you the sort of assurance that'll satisfy you,' Alec said straightforwardly. 'You know I can't. I won't name names, unless it comes to court. That's all I'll say.'

'And if you lock Kerim up for Tracy's death—only you won't, of course—what then? A little bird told me, Your Honour? I found it written on a piece of paper on a rubbish tip, Your Honour? Or, a nightclub hostess told me, and by the way, her name is Sandra. Believe me, Kerim repays his debts.' She waited for Alec's response, his excuse, his persuasion. He said nothing, and a glimmer of a smile formed on her lips.

'Okay, copper, you ask, and if I feel like it, I'll tell you.'

It was slow work, and as they laboured on it became
disappointingly clear that what Sandra knew would add
relatively little to the sum of their information about Kerim.
The only positive gain was the confirmation that Tracy had
indeed been recruited from Mervyn Link's studio to help
the parties along, and had attended three or four.

'Nothing nasty, copper,' Sandra said firmly. 'No floor
shows, no special services. They're big money, these do's.
People with money come to them. Not famous people. Just
rich.'

Most, it seemed, were foreigners, Middle Eastern and,
increasingly, Japanese. Kerim himself invariably acted as
host.

'I heard about a girl called Francesca,' Alec said. 'A girl
who crossed Kerim, and came to a bad end.'

'I dare say you did. But Tracy didn't cross him, did she?
She played her part like a good girl.'

'She didn't enjoy it much, all the same,' Alec said. 'If she
decided she'd had enough, would anyone try and stop her?'

The girl shrugged and lit a cigarette. 'Probably not. So
long as she planned on keeping her mouth shut.'

'But you've stayed the course,' Alec remarked curiously.

'It pays. Maybe I like the company, who knows? Maybe
I'm just getting too old and too sagging to take my clothes
off these days. A girl has to earn a living. There are worse
ways.'

Privately, Alec thought she had probably tried those, too.
He couldn't see too many scruples holding her back. He
watched while she tilted her head and blew smoke at the
ceiling. The visit hadn't been fruitful; not worth the strain
of his meeting with Martine. As a long shot, he said, 'You
didn't know anything about her boyfriends? None of them
chased her around after she'd ditched them?'

Sandra's eyes descended to meet his. 'I wouldn't like you
to get the impression that Tracy and me were bosom pals,
copper,' she said tightly. 'Girls like that don't agree with

me these days. Young girls. Young attractive, innocent girls.'

'I'm not asking whether she wept on your shoulder,' he said roughly. 'Do you know, or don't you?'

'Which one are we talking about? The fancy boy? Or the London lad?'

'You tell me,' Alec said impassively.

Sandra looked at him and shrugged, stubbing her cigarette out in an overflowing ashtray. 'She wanted rid of the fancy boy, the one with the Italian name. I never met him. The other one she ought to have dumped, but she hadn't the heart. Too soft. See what I mean about these young kids? They make me puke.'

'But you met him.'

'I didn't say so. All right, I met him. Nothing to write home about. Should've laid off the beer, but he'd never have got into the movies. They'd been kicking around together for a year or two.'

'Lovers?'

'Not him. He's the sort that can't believe women ever crap because it spoils the image.'

'So when did you last see him?' Alec asked with a casualness which, he realized, Sandra was quick to penetrate. She seemed to weigh the desirability of answering, but in the end, she said, 'Sunday. Last week she was done in, right? Well, he was here the Sunday before. He came to call for her, took her home. She'd been to one of Kerim's do's, we both had, and she kipped here after. Sunday morning, there he is on the mat like something the cat's left.'

'And she left with him?'

More assessing, more reluctance to give what might be bartered. 'She did,' she said in the end. 'She got her stuff together and she went with him, down to the jolly seaside in his jolly car. For all I know.'

Jumbo White. One casual question, a mere offchance, but it had pulled Jumbo White from the shadows. Jumbo

White with his obsessive standards, his chaste ardour, and his amusement arcade which Tracy had been seen to enter but never seen to leave.

He awoke from his reverie to see Sandra watching him keenly.

'Leave it, copper,' she said. 'Kerim's mob done for her. One more innocent from the country, swallowed up by the big city, right? At least she'll never grow old.'

They rose to leave, and Sandra came to the door of the flat.

'You've had your lot, now, copper. Stay away from me now. I've told you all I can. And stay away from Martine. What's she ever done to you?'

Alec turned and made for the stairs, conscious of Jayne's curious glance. Behind them, the door closed and they heard a muffled burst of coughing and then, half caught, the single ting which the telephone bell makes when you pick up the receiver to dial a number. Alec pursed his lips and started down the stairs.

But the day's travelling was far from over. Alec and Jayne reached the car to find their callsign being broadcast on the radio, and answered it to be told that there was a message waiting for them at the local police station, telexed up from the coast. They drove the few streets swiftly, and when Alec had studied the message he spoke to Pringle on the telephone, at length.

'They've found Ricchi,' he said to Jayne, his hand over the receiver. 'It looks like being a long night. Better nip out and get anything you're going to need, and have them make up a Thermos for us.'

Ricchi, it transpired, had been traced to a cottage in a remote Herefordshire hamlet. His car, tucked under a lean-to, had been spotted by the local constable out on an errand to do with a shotgun licence. Nobody had tipped Ricchi off, and Alec was anxious to keep the local force well away until he and Jayne arrived. He talked at length with the Chief Inspector responsible for the area, and arranged for men to be on hand, but he wanted the approach, and the arrest if there was one, to be done by himself.

Dusk was falling and it began to rain as Alec drew in at a lonely crossroads behind the two police cars. The Chief Inspector, a massive, gaunt man, climbed out of the front car and came over.

'On the left-hand side, about three hundred yards. I'm sending the second car down the lane here. There's a track they can follow to get to the back of the cottage.'

'I don't want him warned,' Alec said. 'If the track goes too close they'd better leave the car and do the rest on foot, if you don't mind, sir.'

'That's all right. We won't lose your man.' The vast figure disappeared into the shadows and the driver manœuvred the leading car up on to the bank. There was a murmur of voices, and the second car reversed and swung off down the lane to the left. Alec glanced at Jayne and she flashed him a small smile.

It was a small, pink-washed cottage, conventionally pretty, huddled by the side of the road. Alec pulled the car across to block the entrance and switched off. The manifold, soothing noises of the countryside took over, and Alec listened keenly for tell-tale sounds of the uniformed police, nodding to himself in satisfaction when he heard none.

Guy Ricchi opened the door with a wry smile, recognition sparking in his eyes as he took in their appearance and glanced along to the car with its tell-tale twin aerials. They walked straight in to a poky, shadowed sitting-room where a lamp burned beside an armchair and a book lay face down on a little table.

'I'm sorry,' Ricchi said directly, gesturing them to a lumpy sofa. 'Have you had a lot of trouble tracking me down?'

'We have, rather,' Alec said mildly.

'Like Greta Garbo, I wanted to be alone. This isn't a bad place for it.'

Alec said, 'You have very accommodating partners.'

'I had leave due. We cover for each other a lot, so it wasn't impossible to come away at short notice.' Ricchi hesitated, and added, 'I expect when they heard of Tracy's death they may have put two and two together. They knew, of course, where I used to work, and it was in the papers that she was a receptionist at the health centre.'

'It was her death that made you come away?'

'Yes, it was.'

'Care to amplify that for me?'

Ricchi flushed, looking very young. Alec saw Jayne watch him compassionately as he drew his thoughts together.

'You know, of course, if you've been doing your job at all, that Tracy and I . . . well, we saw a lot of each other, when I was there as a trainee. Did you ever meet her? No, of course not. But you'll have seen pictures. She really was a very attractive girl, and not just where outward beauty was concerned, if I can put it that way. Lively, and determined, and good fun to be with.'

'And very beautiful.'

'Yes, and that too.'

'And you got much more involved than you had intended?'

'Yes. Certainly much more than she intended, I see that now. I got to be serious about her, as people say. I began to think of permanence, of marriage, of a home together—all the things which are anathema to a girl of nineteen with a future before her.'

'And that led to what?'

'For me, all sorts of hang-ups, of course. I had to accept that I had to share her, and that was hard. It was the worst sort of possessiveness, I dare say. The parts of her life that I couldn't share, I wanted her to drop altogether.'

'You never joined her on one of her trips to London?'

'No.'

So far, Alec suspected Ricchi had told them the truth. A lie seemed inconsistent, and he said, 'You never met Tracy in London? Never went about with her there?'

Ricchi shook his head. 'That's not quite what you asked. I did meet her there, once, although we didn't go together. One weekend things sort of came to a head and I . . . I took off after her. I went down and saw her flatmates, but she wasn't there, she was at some country club near London. So I went to look for her,' he said simply.

'And you found her?'

'Amazingly. I knew roughly where to look, and I used a map and a phone book. I got there about midnight. It was one of those gaudy, trashy places that only look passable in the dark. They let me in on some sort of instant membership. I suppose I looked the sort who wouldn't cause trouble.'

'And did you?'

He sighed. 'No. Not in that way. Only trouble for Tracy. I don't suppose she enjoyed that evening very much.'

'I don't suppose you did, either,' Alec murmured.

'It wasn't very good for the ego.' Ricchi's eyes clouded as he looked back at that evening. Out of the corner of his eye, Alec saw Jayne's gaze resting on the young doctor and realized grimly that she was not unsusceptible to this handsome young man with his Latin good looks and his touching tale. Perhaps it was that which made Alec brusque as he asked what had followed the events of that night.

'Nothing, except a coming to terms with the facts of life on my part. I knew, that night, that I was a back number where Tracy was concerned. She made that plain. Cruel to be kind. Don't girls learn that at their mother's knee? I came back to the practice, tried to pull my life together and forget about her. Not to ring her, not to write. I took other girls out and tried to behave badly to them, to blot Tracy out. It was worse because I had seen her in the company of her friends at that club. They were a good crowd,' he said wistfully, 'one she had the entrée to and I didn't, and she was happy with them, you could see that. She didn't need me. She had her own life and I wasn't part of it.'

'So you put her out of your mind?'

'So far as I could.'

'Who told you she was dead? It didn't make the national news until Thursday's papers.'

Ricchi looked at him with the ghost of a smile. 'You mean, how was it that I was so quick off the mark in hiding myself away?'

'If you like.'

'To tell the truth, someone rang me. That's how I found out.'

'Who?'

'Sybil Buxted from the health centre. She didn't like Tracy, and Tracy didn't like her, but she wanted to save me the pain of hearing from someone else. That wasn't untypical of Sybil, though you might not think it to speak to her.'

'And you downed tools and left.'

'Not at once. Sybil rang on Tuesday afternoon. By Wednesday morning I just felt I had to get away to come to terms with it.' He smiled ruefully. 'And tomorrow I go back. I've spoken with my partners this evening on the telephone. Episode closed.'

'It's hardly as simple as that, Dr Ricchi, is it? You're being disingenuous. If Tracy was murdered, you must know you're a suspect.'

'I could hardly kill her if I was a hundred miles away.'

'Can you prove that?'

'Well, for a start you know that I was at home when Sybil rang. Most of the day I spent working on my car. Ask the neighbours. There's not much they miss, I can assure you.'

Jayne's pencil, which had been hurrying over the pages, came to a halt and she looked up. He met her eye. 'Do I seem very foolish? It's not a very edifying spectacle, is it? Unrequited passion.'

'No more foolish than people usually are when they fall in love,' Alec said shortly. The doctor's eyes were still turned appealingly to Jayne, and it was hard to imagine that he would be long inconsolable over Tracy's death. Irritated, Alec stood up, and Jayne followed him to the door.

'End of mystery,' said Jayne as they waited at the cross-roads for the other car to reappear. 'I must say, I feel rather sorry for him. It's hard to give devotion and have it rejected. But then, devotion is not easy to take.'

'You know, of course,' Alec said sarcastically. Jayne coloured, and looked at him.

'I didn't mean I knew it from experience,' she said in a small voice.

'You're right, all the same,' Alec said, angry with himself for the gibe and seeking to make amends. 'As to whether it's the end of our involvement with Ricchi, that depends on whether his story can be substantiated. Speaking selfishly, I'd far rather we had some excuse to arrest him right now, but that won't do. Any arrest isn't good enough —we want the murderer.'

'I thought his story rang true.'

'Yes,' Alec said drily. 'He's a very persuasive character.'

Jayne giggled unexpectedly. 'Sorry. I was just remembering his remark about what girls learn at their mothers' knee. If we learn anything, I'm sure it's to watch out for plausible foreign types with melting eyes and a hard-luck story.' She hesitated, and went on more soberly, 'Tracy Ashford's made a bit of an impression on you, hasn't she, sir?'

'I'm afraid she has. I think she'd have been fun to know. But I can't help feeling sorry for her, too, and not just because she's dead. Consequently, I'm well motivated to find her killer. Plenty of people seem to think she got no more than she deserved, but I can't help seeing it rather differently. And by all accounts she did have a splendid physical presence.'

'That,' said Jayne daringly, 'is just the way I should have expected you to express it.' And the Chief Inspector turned from the radio microphone in bewilderment as first one, then the other of them began to chuckle and their laughter rose and bubbled on the night air.

CHAPTER 11

'So Ricchi stays on the list.'

'It seems so, sir.'

Alec and the Super sat in the latter's office at the county police headquarters. Alec felt stale after the events of the night before and the long drive back to the coast, and had difficulty marshalling his thoughts.

'The latest Ricchi was seen was just after ten, when the woman next door left to take her kid to play group. We already knew that. That leaves Ricchi ample time to get down here by one, which is the earliest Tracy could have died, because of the sightings we have of her up to that time. He could have killed her at any time up to two-thirty, and still have been back home to receive Sybil Buxted's phone call just after five.'

'And what's his motive? Why should he kill her? He'd had six months at least to get over her.'

'I don't know sir. I'm sorry, but I don't know what to think this morning, or even if I'm capable of thinking at all. Maybe it was Ricchi that Tracy had arranged to meet, and she somehow taunted him.'

'Hm. I'm not happy with this reliance on her having an appointment. And this notion of her dressing provocatively, we've no more than the Buxted woman's suggestion that it was because of someone she was going to meet. It was a hot

day, for heaven's sake. Why shouldn't the girl dress as
briefly as she could? All right, we have a number of people
who could have killed her—so far as opportunity goes. But
there's no motive, is there?'

'Henderson and Ricchi had been thrown over by her.
Richardson had been humiliated. Unless maybe she was
trying a bit of blackmail on him, too.'

'That's a bit more like it. That's what I'd call a motive.
And Richardson's quite powerful enough physically to have
drowned her. Which Henderson, for example, probably
isn't.'

'What about White? I know he was supposed to be on
the pier all day, sir, but it's still our last sighting of the girl.'

The older man swivelled in his chair to look out of the
window across the trees. 'Have another go at White,' he
said at last. 'Alibis are made to be broken, after all. But I
want the pressure kept up on Richardson. Maybe she was
into blackmail. We know there was something, something
he's not too keen to talk about, between him and the girl.
Check at the headland car park again in case someone
remembers his car, or him. Find out from his office staff
whether his hair was damp when he came back to the office
last Tuesday. If need be, we'll go over his car for traces of
sand. When you've done all that, we'll have him in and give
him another grilling on our own ground.'

The interview seemed to be over, but Alec hesitated. The
other man swung back in his chair. 'Well?'

'What about the London end, sir? Isn't it still the most
likely solution that Kerim had one of his men settle a score?
Who else was she in contact with who is known to have
been associated with a killing?'

'The word is,' the Super said heavily, 'that Kerim Halfaya
is not to be harried unless we are certain beyond all reasonable doubt that he was, himself, personally, Tracy's murderer. And even then we are merely to put the facts before
a Higher Power who will consider what action to take. If

any.' He stared at Alec, defying him to protest.

Alec stared back, for a moment doubting the evidence of his ears. 'That's that, then,' he said at length. Foreigners could get away with almost anything in this country, he thought bitterly, if they were influential enough. Even, literally, murder. What was Tracy Ashford's death, after all, to some Foreign Office mandarin weighing up the pros and cons of a diplomatic incident? One dead pin-up model in the balance against a hypothetical and unquantifiable effect on the country's trade with a single nation. There was no doubt which side the scales would come down.

'If it's any comfort,' the Super said, 'I doubt if Kerim had anything to do with it. Tracy Ashford was pretty small fry, after all is said and done, in his terms. What real damage could she have done him? She was no threat. I doubt whether he had her killed.'

Alec drove despondently back to the little seaside town, left his car at the police station and wandered down to the front. Somewhere here, a week ago, Tracy had died. Nothing had changed; even the tide was much as it had been then. He watched the sunbathers thronging the beach, the pedaloes shuffling to and fro, the little mounds of clothes left islanded on the sand, the idlers watching from the pier. Was it really possible that murder had been committed here, under the cloak of playfulness? A cool and determined killer might have achieved it. Far out, where the keenest swimmers could just be seen as little dots among the waves, it might have been possible to press a girl under the surface and hold her there, possible even to remove her swimming costume—but why? And what then? The killer could hardly emerge from the waters clutching a bikini in his hands. It had to have been the Haven, then. Alec gazed dazedly round at the myriads of figures on the beach and in the sea. How could he find a murderer among so many? Suppose Tracy had gone for a quiet swim on her own and met someone in the water that they knew nothing of? Or even a total stranger?

He recalled the enthusiasm of the girl at the country club for making love in the water. Had horseplay developed into something more? Had the clutch of sexual embrace tightened convulsively into the fatal grip of murder?

He became conscious of a voice speaking his name, and turned to see Heather standing watching him in quiet concern.

'Sorry. Have you been trying to catch my attention?'

'You were miles away.'

He smiled an apology. 'You look nice.' And indeed she did, cool and colourful in skirt and blouse and sandals. Instinctively, he looked about him for her companion.

'Cathy's having her hair done. Come and have an ice-cream.'

'I ought to get back.'

'Not yet. You'll work all the better for having something first. Come on.' And Alec found himself following her into an ice-cream parlour, where they sat at the back in the shade and ordered sundaes, and soon he began to tell her about the frustrations of the case. He talked in general terms, and she asked for no details and no names, but he spoke of the country club, and the fruitless travelling, and his fear that he never would be able to bring anyone into the dock for Tracy Ashford's death. At the end he apologized for boring her with his troubles. He said nothing of Jayne.

'You haven't bored me.' They sat companionably picking at their ice-creams and Alec began to feel happier. 'You've been here ten days,' he said. 'A week since we met on the sands.'

'I know. We leave on Saturday. It's a shame, isn't it? Just when we're getting to know you.'

Alec said, 'I'd like to spend another evening with you both before the end of your holiday. It's been a comfort to know there was somewhere I could go to unwind. I'm only sorry I've been too busy to come more often.'

'Do come. Cathy would love you to, and I . . . I'd like it,

too.' She hesitated, looking down at the table and toying with the empty sundae glass. 'I might be able to stay a little longer. If I took another week's leave. I don't suppose they'd mind that much. Of course, I'd have to stay somewhere else. There'll be new people in the apartment on Saturday.' She looked up and searched his face seriously. 'If it would help,' she said, 'to have someone around.'

Alec said gently, 'That's very kind of you. Don't you think it might be a mistake, though? Even another week would come to an end. And I might be here much longer than that. It wouldn't be right to risk your job.'

'I dare say you're right. It was just an idea. Well,' she added brightly, 'I'd better let you get back.'

'Does the offer still stand, to call round one evening?'

She looked at him curiously. 'If you like.'

'I would like to.' He led the way through the shop to the pavement. They shook hands rather formally and parted, and Alec made his way to the police station with mixed feelings. First Martine, now Heather. Why was it that when you felt only affection and gratitude for people, you ended up hurting them all the same?

Alec spent the afternoon sifting through the reports on his desk, reviewing his tactics in the light of the last few days' developments and trying to juggle the limited manpower to the best effect. Privately, he had determined that he would continue to include Kerim Halfaya in his inquiry, albeit with a certain amount of discretion. If at the end of the day he had to draw back, at least he would have satisfied his own mind as much as he could.

Increasingly, he was beginning to feel that there must be factors he had overlooked altogether, and that once the immediate suspects were eliminated he would have to make a fresh start on totally different lines. With this in mind, he spent two hours at the end of the afternoon cross-questioning Tracy's father about his daughter's home life, and followed it up with a second interview with the three students with whom Tracy had shared the house.

'Which all gets us no further forward at all,' he complained to John Pringle as they walked back down through the town. 'If only we could find some way in which the killing could have occurred elsewhere.'

'Could she have been taken out in a boat?' Pringle asked.

'I thought of that one. Liz Pink is checking the hire boats, and talking to the fishermen. They'd have to go a good long way out, for the murderer to be sure that they wouldn't be seen by someone with binoculars on the headland, or from one of the telescopes on the promenade. I shouldn't have thought it's terribly easy to drown someone when you're in a boat, but it must be possible. Ditto taking their clothes off once they're dead.'

'It would account for the bruising after death, though, sir. If the body was alongside the boat and the murderer was leaning over trying to strip her clothes off.'

'True. Or if they were a fair way out, she might have taken her things off to sunbathe. It mucks up the timescale, though, doesn't it? The boat hire places are all a goodish way from the pier, where she was seen at one or thereabouts; then you have to allow for the time to get out to sea and— since Tracy couldn't have foreseen that it was going to be a one-way trip—the time to get back. All before she was due back at work at two-thirty.'

'It's a poser, sir. If she was stunned first, she could have been pushed out of a boat easily enough, or even dropped from a helicopter, but what about the pathologist's report and the marks of fingers on the back of her neck? Someone was definitely alongside her, holding her under.'

'And that still leaves us with Richardson, White, Ricchi and Henderson and the ridiculous unlikelihood of her going for a friendly swim with any of them. Which of them is it, John?'

'I only wish I knew, sir.'

Later that evening, Alec and Jayne strolled together along the front before making their way to the hotel. The hours of reports and papers and more reports had been wearying in the oppressive heat of the old police station and it was pleasant to linger in the cooler air before returning to the hotel. The suck and wash of the surf soothed them, and muted the garish noise of the booths and amusements.

Jayne, with her sensitivity to when they could and could not speak as friends rather than colleagues, asked, 'Is it making it harder for you, having me here, Alec?'

He thought for a moment before answering. 'In some ways. But I'm glad you've come. It's always easier to work with people you know from past cases,' he added, but he knew that wasn't the truth. It had been easy, when he sat on the beach at the start of his holiday, or later as he passed his time with Heather and Cathy, or Martine, to imagine that he was weaning himself from his attachment to Jayne quite successfully; but with her here beside him he knew that was not true. He was as much in thrall to her as ever, and the idea of getting free was merely an irrelevance. She was the person who had attracted his love and he could only come to terms with that, not alter it.

Perhaps something of what was passing through Alec's mind showed in his face, for Jayne said quietly, 'I'm glad circumstances have brought us back together, Alec. I wouldn't have wanted us to drift apart with bad feeling.'

'You never gave way to bad feeling,' he said ruefully. 'It was me that found it hard to be crossed. I'm too used to being in charge.'

'I like you for it. And I enjoy your company, Alec. I was sorry things developed the way they did.'

They came to the pier end where the entrance signs and ticket booths cast a pool of yellow light and in unspoken accord turned towards the booths. Alec bought them tickets, and they emerged on the echoing boards of the pier as on to the reverse of a cinema set. The wash of the sea swirled beneath the gaps in the timbers.

'Couldn't we try again?' Alec asked tentatively. 'Don't you think we could work something out?'

'Could we?' she said, turning her head to him, and her face was calm and, he thought, a little sad. 'Don't you think a re-run of last time would be rather hard to bear?'

'You won't change your mind?'

'Live with you? No, I won't.'

'Your religious scruples?'

'If you like. My scruples.'

'Well, I wish I understood them,' Alec said bitterly. 'Are you sure they're not just a pretty way of making me jump to your tune? I suppose your mother told you never to let a man have his way with you until you've chained him to the altar. Do me the justice of taking my feeling for you seriously, can't you?'

'Don't say any more, Alec.'

'Yes, but this isn't the nineteenth century, Jayne, for Christ's sake. So don't be so damned righteous about it all.'

'Alec, leave it,' she said anxiously, but Alec was too wound up to heed her, or to heed his own sense, and all his frustrations with the case, all his physical and mental tiredness, poured bitterly out in his denunciation of her reticence.

'Ricchi was right about you women learning things at your mothers' knee,' he finished bitingly, 'but in your case what you've learnt was the worst sort of priggish hypocrisy.'

'Leave my mother out of this,' Jayne snapped with unexpected fire. 'If you choose to see my actions as hypocritical and priggish I can't stop you. But you say I'm to do you justice. Well, do me the justice to consider that my scruples, as you call them, may just possibly be hard to keep to, and may mean more to me than even the love of Alec Stainton. I won't be bullied, Alec, and I thought I knew you better than to think you'd try. That's why we can't begin all over again. Because I won't change and you can't.'

Their footsteps mocked them hollowly as they walked in uneasy silence along the pier, in and out of the pools of light. Through the cracks in the timbers Alec glimpsed the oily glint of the sea. Eventually they came to the far end, where the pavilion sat out the winter gales with its little theatre where the once-famous names played out their declining years, its fish and chip restaurant, the arcades, and the hidden, empty storerooms and cellars, beneath which were only the waves. Canned music, the echo of electronic games, and the squeals of children met them and they walked on to the very end where elderly couples and young lovers sat in silent pairs on the damp benches. Spray whipped around them as they leant side by side against the ornate railing, gazing out to sea where every half-minute a lighthouse flashed its cryptic sequence.

At last Alec turned and leant back against the railings, and made his voice light. 'Fancy a bag of chips?'

'It doesn't seem so warm out here, does it?' It was an olive branch, and she grasped it thankfully. 'Mind if I go and find the loo while you get them?'

They arranged to meet back where they were, and Alec wended his way to the chip restaurant, a warm, greasy island of light. Despite queuing, he was back at the rendezvous before Jayne, who returned smelling pungently of soap.

'Sorry about the rather sanitary smell,' she said, and Alec was relieved to see her normal smile, if a little wan, reappear. 'That's what took me so long. It's some stuff they use with salt water, but it takes ages to get a lather up.'

'Have a chip,' Alec began, and then, turning to her, as he took in what she had said, 'What was that again?'

'I said I was sorry I was so long . . .'

'No, after that. About the soap.'

'Only that it's special stuff for use in salty water. They must . . . oh, Alec.'

'Here.' Alec thrust the bag of chips at her. 'Eat these before they get cold. I'll be back in a minute.'

But Jayne, the implications of what she had said ringing bells of warning and victory in her head, hurried after him, and put a hand on his elbow to guide him.

'Down these stairs,' she said. 'The Ladies' is on this side. I expect there's a Gentlemen's the far side in the same place.'

'See if you can trace where it comes from. The water, I mean.' He left her still clutching the soggy bag of chips and crossed through the amusement arcade, out to the walkway on the far side where the entrance to the lavatory was. Inside, he made for the washbasins and turned the cold tap. The water was salty on his fingertips, and when he stood on the lavatory seat in one of the cubicles and reached a hand into the cistern, the water there was saline too. Eagerly, he found the supply pipe and traced it back as far as he could, but it vanished into the wall on the arcade side of the room and he hurried back into the arcade and hunted for the pipe, only to find that it disappeared from view after only a few inches.

'Have a chip,' Jayne's voice said beside him. 'It's a shame to waste them.'

Alec looked at her, then took a cool chip from the greasy wrapping. Around them, children and adults drifted from game to game, while the sharp crack of the rifles in the shooting gallery punctuated the clamour. Across the room, Alec caught sight of his own reflection in the mirror, and he remembered Jumbo White, hunched behind the one-way glass, surveying his domain.

'Come on,' he said to Jayne. 'Don't rush, but it's time we went.' They turned towards the stairs again, and Jayne took his arm as they climbed to the upper deck. Once there, they quckened their pace back towards the distant esplanade.

'Who'd have the plans?' Alec asked, thinking aloud.

'Water authority? Not if they're using sea water. Borough engineer?'

'Why the rush?'

'White. He was watching us.'

'How? The mirrors?'

'One-way glass,' Alec confirmed. 'Richardson never met her, although it was him she was dressed for, to turn the screw of his humiliation. Randy old goat, that's how she'd see him. But she never got as far as the headland. She never left the pier.'

'But what about the clothes? And surely someone would have seen?'

'Maybe.'

'I suppose it is half a mile from the beach. All the same . . .'

'Got it. Rating authority.'

'Sir?' Unconsciously, they were both back on the job.

'Who has the plans of every building in a town? The people who collect the rates. It's all on a square footage basis. So there have to be plans.' Memories of a grim night in Northern Ireland swam in and out of his mind, of a raid on a warehouse where a wanted man was hiding out, and of the pencilled plan and the tubby civil servant, blinking in the lights of the police compound, telling them over and over that it was the only copy and he mustn't let it out of his sight or they'd never be able to work out the rates. Memories, too, of the tension, and the fear, and the long wait, and the two shots that echoed and rolled round the cavernous warehouse. And of the long, weary session with the Intelligence Officer, and the police, and his own CO, that went on until the wan daylight overcame the glare of the neon.

Alec hurried along the front at Rifle Brigade pace, Jayne taking little running steps every now and then to keep up. Once she asked, 'Won't it wait until tomorrow?'

'Ten to one it would,' Alec replied shortly. 'We can't

afford the one chance.' They kept up their cracking pace, up the main street towards the square in the town centre, almost deserted, and right up the steps of the police station.

'Who's in?' Alec asked the desk sergeant economically.

'Inspector Farmer, sir. And WPC Pink. Detective-Sergeant Pringle and your chap, Johnson, have both gone home.'

'Get them back here soonest. I'll be with the Inspector. Come on, Jayne.'

Inspector Farmer, busy with personnel reports, was not unhappy to be disturbed, and reading the urgency of the situation in Alec's face became at once businesslike and alert. He listened while Alec briefly stated the facts, then lifted the phone and spoke first to the desk sergeant, then to County HQ. Then he crossed to a filing cabinet and leafed through until he came to a copy of the post-mortem report on Tracy Ashford, scanning it swiftly before passing it to Alec.

'It fits. The pathologist was never very happy with the idea of her body being battered by rocks after it went into the sea. But from what I understand of what's written there, the injuries are quite consistent with her being washed around the pier legs. See this, too.' He leant over and pointed at a paragraph. 'Chips in the stomach. And there. Bruising on the forehead, just a few minutes before death. We wondered how that came there.'

The phone on Farmer's desk rang. He picked it up, then handed the receiver to Alec. 'Your boss,' he said. Jayne listened as Alec outlined the situation, and her eyes widened as he spoke again, and she caught Inspector Farmer's eye.

'He's coming down,' Alec said, replacing the receiver.

'I'm very glad to hear it. We'd better get weaving while he's on his way.'

The telephone rang again, strangled immediately as Farmer snatched it up. 'Johnson's in,' he said, cupping a hand over the mouthpiece. 'You want him down at the pier?'

'Yes. He knows White. There's only the one way off.'

'Unless he wants to swim for it.'

'Put Johnson at the ticket turnstile. Have you anyone else within reach?'

'I'll keep a car within range.' He turned back to the phone and relayed his orders, economical and authoritative.

Jayne said, 'Can't we pick him up quietly? As he comes off the pier?'

For once, Alec had forgotten her presence. He turned to her. 'Possibly. But we have to assume he knows we're on to him, and he's a nutter where guns are concerned, don't forget. What if he grabs a holidaymaker as hostage, or looses off at all and sundry? And once he's off the pier, we could have a job finding him, let alone picking him up safely.'

'On the other hand,' Inspector Farmer said, putting the phone down, 'going about things as we are, there's a risk we will actually trigger off an over-reaction on his part. If he sees us coming in mob-handed it may be just enough to set him reaching for the gun cupboard. Alec thinks we have to take that chance. More important, so does the Superintendent.' He frowned. 'All the same, I wish this chap from the rates office would hurry up. If we've jumped to the wrong conclusion we'll have wasted a lot of time and effort.'

As if in answer to his words, there was a knock at the door and WPC Pink appeared to say that the rating officer was outside with a colleague.

'Shoot them in,' Farmer said.

The rating officer might have been formed to confound the image of the unassertive petty official beloved of script-writers. Large, rubicund, good-humoured, he brushed aside Inspector Farmer's apologies for interrupting his evening and introduced his colleague.

'This is the chap with the gen,' he said genially. 'This is

the chap who does the work. All we do is collect the dough so that our beloved councillors can spend it on swimming pools and fairy lights and keeping dogs on a lead. If it's plans and details you're after, these are the boys who have them.'

His colleague, quiet and courteous, fished in a briefcase and brought out a green file, bulging with papers, new, old, yellowing, fastened with a tag which he struggled with as he spoke. 'As Jack says, we're the ones who actually work out rateable values. Of course, the pier is rather old, and therefore so are our plans. And as alterations and additions have been made, rather than redraw the whole plan, they've been added on separate sheets. However—' he succeeded at last in extracting the tag— 'this should tell you most of what you want to know.' Alec and Inspector Farmer leant eagerly over the plan which he spread carefully over the Inspector's desk.

'I wish we had the resources to make plans as carefully as this these days,' the man said sadly, and indeed, even Jayne, leaning forward from where she sat, could see that it was meticulously prepared, on thick linen paper with careful hatching and colour-washing and fine, spidery captions. 'This is the top storey,' the man went on. 'This one's the middle—that's the arcade, there, and the theatre—and this is the lowest level.'

'Right,' Alec said. 'I see. This must be the room where I talked to our man,' he said to Farmer. 'And these are the lavatories. The thing we're especially interested in,' he explained to the two officials, 'is the arrangement for water supplies to the lavatories and so on. Would these plans show that?'

'Hum. If my memory serves me right, they use sea water, don't they?'

'That's right,' the big man agreed heartily. 'Pumped up to a big tank on the roof of the theatre.'

'Into the roof?' Alec asked in dismay.

'Naturally. You have to have a good head of water. You have a tank in the roof of your house for the same reason.'

The valuer delved into the green file again. 'I fancy we have a separate plan of the plant and equipment. Yes, here we are.' Alec pored over the drawing as he traced it out with his finger. 'That's the tank, you see. This line, then, is the outflow to the lavatories in the arcade, and also to the theatre itself and the restaurant. This is the inlet, and it comes up from the bottom deck. It's mostly stores and so on down there, disused for the most part. It looks as if there's a separate tank here. It may be that it is too far to pump water up from the sea in one go—low tide level, of course—so it's done in two stages. Now I think of it, I remember seeing it years ago when I went over the whole pier updating our records. Is that any help?'

Alec looked at Farmer, who nodded grimly. He turned back to the valuer. 'One other point, while we're about it. Is there any chance that there's some sort of chute for discharging rubbish into the sea?'

Both officials shook their heads. 'It wasn't that they were too worried what went into the sea,' the rating officer said. 'But they wouldn't have wanted to offend the visitors by the sight of a shower of rubbish or sewage descending from beneath their precious pier—or risk having it wash up on to the beach. No, they built a little tramway, actually, for hauling rubbish back to the promenade. It's quite a feature. One of the things the pier's famous for. But,' he added, watching Alec's face keenly, 'if what you're asking, is whether there's any way of getting down to sea level without being visible from the beach, then nothing's easier. You just go down the stairs.'

'Stairs?'

'Here.' The valuer put another plan in front of Alec. 'Inside the pier legs. One beneath the theatre basement and one under the stores beneath the amusement arcade. You go down a spiral stair—it's pretty damp and dark, but I've done it myself. You come out on to a little platform above high tide level, and then there's a ladder to get you down to your boat or whatever.' Jayne noticed that the eyes of both men were bright, and it was clear that the import of what they were saying was not lost on them.

Inspector Farmer picked up the phone and cupped his hand over the mouthpiece. 'Mind if we copy these?' he asked briefly.

'Please do. I was hoping you wouldn't want the originals. You've no idea how much work it would take to replace them.'

'And thank you both for your help. If you'd just like to wait outside, we'll let you have the plans back directly, and in the meantime we'll have them fetch you a cup of tea. We'd rather you kept quiet about all this for the time being, please.'

And the two men, with a brief glance which suggested there was not much they hadn't guessed, gathered up their things and went out.

CHAPTER 12

'The question is,' Inspector Farmer said, turning to Alec after the two men had gone, 'why did he strip her?'

'I don't know,' said Alec slowly. 'At least, I don't know for sure. Who can say for certain how a man's mind works when he is on the point of committing murder? Maybe we'll find the truth from White after we've got him. I fancy the answer may lie in the realm of the psychiatrist rather than the policeman.'

'The clothes went the same way as the body, of course: weighted down to stop them drifting ashore.'

'I guess so. Or they may be hoarded somewhere in the storerooms beneath the arcade.'

'But why kill her at all?' Jayne asked. 'What possible reason could he have for wanting her dead? He loved her.' Farmer looked at her meditatively. 'You mean,' she said, 'because he loved her he wanted to save her from herself.'

'Something like that, I think,' Alec replied. 'It was the only way to put a stop to her doing the things he couldn't accept—the photo sessions, the nightclub work, the drugs, maybe.'

'It still seems a pretty thin reason to kill a girl,' Jayne said dismally. But was it, she thought, in fact so far from the way someone like White, so limited in his view of women, might behave? What had Sandra said? He was the sort who couldn't believe women ever crap because it spoils the image. She smiled briefly to herself. It was true. She had come across men like that.

'It lets Richardson out,' Inspector Farmer was saying. 'I don't like that man. The town could do without him.'

'He employs a great many people.'

'The ultimate holiness. Well, I'd better start to marshal the troops.'

'Mm. White knows that pier, that's what makes me cautious. He knew about the water tank, and the stairs. What else is there down there that he knows about and we don't?'

Farmer said, 'There's only one way on or off, unless he wants to swim for it. And even that we can cover with a boat, and a man on the beach.'

Alec said, 'Who here is cleared for firearms?'

'I am.' Farmer frowned. 'And John Pringle is not long back from the refresher course. I don't like firearms very much, Alec. I've tried very hard to keep them out of this town and so far I've succeeded.'

Alec shool his head. 'I'd like to agree with you, but White, out there, proves you wrong, with his rifles and his Luger that Rommel used.'

'Amusement arcade stuff. Militaria.'

'A man who loves guns sooner or later wants the chance to use them. It's the justification of his love, the consummation, if you like. He can't help wondering how it would feel and wanting, one day, to find out.'

'If he knows we're on to him.'

Alec thought of the one-way windows on to the arcade and the gloomy elephantine head weaving and swaying as Jumbo White looked out on his domain. 'He knows,' he said.

There was a hiatus then, so far as Jayne was concerned, until the arrival of the Superintendent an hour and a quarter later. Alec, alone in his room, pored over the plans of the pier and the too-brief list of available officers and roughed out his plan of action. Farmer, in the canteen where major briefings were held seldom enough, pinned plans to walls, arranged for seating to be set out, and kept tabs on the personnel state as the desk sergeant ran through the phone numbers and the patrol cars picked up those who were off duty. Slowly the police station filled up, and Jayne fretted and fidgeted at her own inaction. At one stage she took it on herself to fetch Alec a plastic cup of coffee and a roll, but he barely acknowledged them and she hesitated, then left him alone. She remembered the lecturer at training college, a grizzled warrior who had seen it all and surveyed his pink-faced class with cynical amusement. 'When it happens, it happens so damn quick that you don't know what you're doing. And then, if you haven't trained, trained, trained, you get it wrong. But before that comes the waiting. And believe me, the waiting is the hardest thing.'

It was shortly after eleven o'clock that the waiting ended and Jayne found herself caught up in a blur of activity which she afterwards tried in vain to recall with clarity.

Alec conducted the briefing in the canteen, the Super on one side of him, Farmer on the other. Alec paused before he spoke, gathering up the attention of the men and women waiting on his words as he had, Jayne guessed, in so many briefings in the past in platoon HQs and night leaguers, in barbed-wire-festooned police stations and military posts, in jungle clearings and pine forests. When he spoke, it was with economy and authority. It was, Jayne thought, neither the mild, unassuming Alec she had come to know over the tangled months of their relationship, nor yet the quietly competent detective-inspector she was used to working with, but a cool, almost chillingly detached tactician to whom the success of the operation as planned was the sole justification of their work and for whom she, the attentive constables and sergeants, even Inspectpr Farmer and the Superintendent, were mere units of manpower, with weaknesses and fallibilities to be allowed for, it was true, but no greater human characteristic. Yet curiously she was not repelled. Indeed, watching his tense features, she surprised in herself a yearning to comfort and to mother which was so strong she dug her nails into her palms to stop her crying out as she remembered the vulnerable, dependent, humorous man who withheld with such careful pride from declarations of love.

Maps were passed round, timings written up on the blackboard, questions asked to ensure each man and woman knew their part in the plan. Finally, Alec glanced at the Superintendent, who lumbered to his feet.

'You've heard Detective-Inspector Stainton,' he said, 'and you know about chummy and his little collection of guns. Because of that collection, Detective-Inspector Stainton has asked me for permission for weapons to be issued to trained officers. Chummy likes guns, and people that like them like to use them. Detective-Sergeant Pringle and Detective-Inspector Stainton will have handguns this evening. I don't like that much, and I've told both officers that I don't want them used if there is any alternative at all. I want no pulling off at shadowy figures tonight. If chummy decides to hole up we'll play a waiting game and starve him out. I'm reminding both these officers in the presence of you all that they are not to engage if there is any—and I mean any—alternative. All right. Let's go.'

Walking along the damp boarding of the pier for the second time that night, Jayne felt strangely peaceful. Far below, the waves lapped round the piles and a tangy smell of seaweed seeped through the boards. It was just on midnight; the turnstiles were closed and already lights at the end of the pier were being doused. In the quiet of the night, with the music and the funfairs stilled, it was easy to imagine oneself back in the eighteenth-century fishing village or the decorous Victorian railway resort.

They reached the seaward end of the walkway and in little knots of shadow dispersed, some to watch the stairways, some to the far end by the deserted telescope. Ahead, Alec turned down the stairs to the arcade, Pringle and Inspector Farmer on his heels. Jayne followed, taking up her station at the foot of the stairs, where she could look along the aisles of the fruit machines and computer games, dark and silent, and just make out the silhouette of Liz Pink and the bulk of a uniformed constable at the farther end.

Jayne never saw what happened after Alec knocked on the door of White's office room at the side of the arcade, but she heard the loud challenge Farmer gave, and the splintering of the woodwork and then, simultaneous with the crash of the door being flung back, a louder, heavier explosion which echoed and rolled around the arcade below the ceiling, and an oath.

Slowly, she edged down the dark stairway, feeling with one hand for the wall by her side. There seemed to be some unaccountable obstruction in her throat and she swallowed to get rid of it, but it wouldn't go. So this was what fear was like. A dank, chill air surrounded her as she left the arcade behind and the stairs dog-legged, as if she were descending to the sea bed itself. She felt very much alone.

She began to speak before she got to the foot of the stairs, forcing her voice to be calm, even cheerful, so far as she could. It sounded strained and unnatural, none the less. 'Mr White? It's me, Jayne Simmonds. Did you see me earlier in the evening? I came on to the pier and ate some chips. You run the amusement arcade. I've always enjoyed amusement arcades.'

Silence. Somewhere, a pipe dripped with a heavy 'plunk' into a tank. Tracy Ashford had heard that same sound, she thought with a chill. Was she unconscious before he got her down here, or did he lure her with some pretence? It must have been fully as dark and as dank, for all the sunlight outside, that last day of her life.

'Mr White, I've come to tell you we understand about Tracy. You hated what she was doing, didn't you, but you loved her. You must have grown to love her very much over the years.'

Still no reply, and she resisted an urge to cry out, to say: 'If you're there, say something.' Was that the rustle of clothing? A board creaked as someone shifted their weight, or maybe it was only the pier yielding to the push and suck of the waves.

She fought to keep her voice calm. 'Don't make things hard now, Mr White. It can't help Tracy. You killed her because you loved her, didn't you? You had to stop her doing what she did. Don't kill anyone else. Not now. Not when it won't help Tracy, or anyone.'

All the time she edged forward, forcing her mind to see the plan she had studied of the layout of this dark bottom deck, until she judged she was in the centre of the room. Then she stood still, her eyes as they became accustomed to the dark beginning to separate the darker from the lighter shadows. Over to one side, was that . . .? She looked away, bringing it to the edge of her vision, and knew it was White, ten yards away, against the wall with his back to the door which led to the tank room.

'Come with me, Mr White,' she said more quietly. 'It's over now. Don't begin again.' Behind her she dimly heard a footfall on the stairs and prayed that nothing would push White over the edge into violence and destruction. She waited, and there was silence, and then she picked out White's heavy, laboured breathing. 'I'm going to come over to you, Mr White, and hold out my hand for the gun.' She made herself sound matter of fact, reassuring, but she knew she was trembling and her bladder felt weak. 'Will you give it to me? Will you hold out the gun so that I can take it? I'll look after it for you. I won't let anyone damage it. I know you take care of your collection. Then we must go up to the arcade, where it's light. It's too dark down here. I should be scared if I was on my own.' She nerved herself and began to move slowly towards him.

'I'm coming over to you, Mr White. Can you see me? I'm coming over to fetch the gun, and then we'll both go up into the light again. It's been a long day.'

'No.' The word came out as a cry. 'No. Stay there. I'll use it, I'll use the gun.'

'No, Mr White. I'd better take it, don't you think? You couldn't shoot me. You couldn't shoot Tracy. You loved her too much. You couldn't see her face when she died.'

'Stay there.' The voice was hoarse with tension and she thought: He's going to do it. He's going to go over the top. And she willed the others: Don't move, don't do anything, nothing at all, or he'll pull the trigger.

She was three yards from White, close enough now to see the pale blur of his face and hands, and something else, the dull glint of metal and oil. She could smell the acrid chemical odour of the gun.

'Here I am,' she said. 'I'll take just a few steps more, then you can reach me the gun. I shan't touch you, Mr White. You couldn't bear it when Tracy touched you, could you? And when she touched others, and they gloated over her. That was all wrong. She should be pure, like she was when you first knew her. That was how you wanted her to stay, wasn't it? Just as you first knew her.'

'She din' know what she was doing,' White muttered. ''Ow could she know? When she did those things. When she dressed like a tart. I arst 'er to stop, I tried to tell 'er what men are like, an' their awful desires. There wasn't no uvver way to stop 'er. Somebody 'ad to stop 'er. They'll take me aht an' 'ang me for it, won't they? But I 'ad to do it. Somebody 'ad to stop 'er.'

'They don't hang anybody these days,' Jayne said gently. 'Not any more. Now they understand, they try and help you.' And God knows, she thought, that may be as bad in its way.

'They ought to,' his voice came again, so quietly she had to strain to make out the words. 'Awful desires. There's no uvver way. I've tried.'

'I know,' Jayne said, and took a step forward. 'I know you've tried. To come to terms with it in yourself.'

'I took her clothes off of 'er. I didn't want to. Something made me. I just wanted ter look. I didn't do nuffing to 'er.'

'You wanted to look at her beauty.'

'That's it. That's it. Not like the uvvers. Not dirty, not perverted.'

'And she was very beautiful.' Jayne took another step, and now she was no more than a foot or two from White and the gun, unwavering, was close enough to reach out and grab, but it pointed straight at her heart.

'Will you give me the gun? Mr White? There's no more you can do for Tracy now.'

'She was beautiful,' White said, so low that Jayne strained to catch the words. 'Only, then she woke up.'

Slowly, watching his eyes, she reached out for the gun. Her fingers touched the warm metal, and she edged them inch by inch along the barrel to take the weight. Then there was a sob, convulsive and racking, and the gun jerked from

her grasp and she lunged for it desperately as the barrel
glinted and she saw what was going to happen. At the last
moment she cried out and slapped hard at his arm with the
flat of her hand at full stretch and then the world exploded
in light and noise and violence and she was knocked to
the ground, her breath beaten out of her. Someone was
struggling on top of her and a voice cried 'There,' and then
she was being rolled to one side and the room was full of
light and people and Alec was bending over her, a gun in
his hand, and the acrid stench of it reached her and she
turned aside and retched bitterly.

Alec held her head and when she was better pressed his
handkerchief into her hand. She turned back to see the room
full of people, and the Superintendent cautioning White who
stood, crying, between two constables. Detective-Sergeant
Pringle came over with a plastic bag and gingerly took the
reeking gun from Alec's hand.

'Better?' Alec asked, and she managed a wan smile.

'A little.' He helped her to her feet and she pulled her
clothes straight. Her cheek felt bruised, and the palm of
her hand was red and sore where she had slapped at the
gun.

'Well done,' he said, and she was unreasonably glad at
such uneffusive praise.

'I just said the first thing that came into my head.'

'It was perfect.'

'He was going to kill himself, wasn't he?' Jayne said, in
a voice which wouldn't quite stay level.

'Yes. The bullet went into the ceiling.'

'Poor White.'

'Poor Tracy. If she'd only worn something different that
day, instead of setting out to provoke Richardson, she might
be alive still. It was her skimpy sun top which finally pushed
White over the edge.'

'So he knocked her out?'

'It was the only way he knew to make the chance to take

her clothes off her. I expect he's right. He only wanted to look. How can we tell what goes on inside a mind that's unbalanced?'

'And then she woke up.'

'And he panicked, and they fought. Maybe he knocked her out again before dragging her into the tank room and drowning her. The doctors may tell us that, or White may. Then he carried her body down the stairway inside the pier-leg and simply watched it float away.'

'It's sordid, Alec, isn't it?'

'It's depressing. Not the way you'd like a young girl's life to end. White had a poor opinion of men and their affections, and heaven knows, there's reason enough. But he had too high an opinion of women. The old conflict between the angel and the whore. That's why Tracy died, ultimately.' He put an arm round her and helped her to the stairs. Already, they were almost alone, a single constable standing at the stairhead, the rest of the cast of the night's drama down at the far end of the arcade, where the reflection of a blue light told of a waiting car on the upper deck.

'Where are we going?' Jayne asked as they started on the long walk back to the land.

'You're going back to the hotel, Jayne. Miss Helston will put you to bed. I'm going back to the station. I'll see you in the morning.'

They walked together along the deserted front. Jayne said, 'I'm glad we didn't have to use guns. Aren't you?'

'I'm always glad when we don't have to.'

'Are you?' she asked idly. Don't you sometimes find in yourself that same urge you talked about in White—the urge to use a gun, because it's there?'

Alec was silent, and she wondered if she had trespassed too far on forbidden ground. 'Yes,' he said at last. 'That's how I knew he would be tempted.'

Jayne moved closer to him and slipped her hand into his. It was no time to think of complications and misunderstandings between them. 'You'll go and see those two girls tomorrow? Heather and Cathy? There's still a few days of your holiday left.'

He threw back his head and laughed silently. 'What's so funny?' she demanded.

'Your innocent concern. And your estimation of me. You must think men very shallow creatures. You've no idea, have you, how I felt when I watched you start down those stairs to talk to White.'

'I do know what you said to the Superintendent when he suggested White would probably respond better to a woman. You were very rude to him, Alec.'

'If anything had happened to you I'd probably have shot him on the spot.'

Jayne pondered his words, uncertain whether she liked such an open avowal of his care for her. 'Yes, but about Heather and Cathy. Do go and see them. If not for your sake, then for theirs.'

'If you like.'

'And the other girl. The nightclub hostess.'

Alec thought of Martine's packed, ephemeral life, her knowingness and her innocence, and knew he could do nothing for her except stay out of her life. And what would that life be in five, in ten years, when her modelling days were past and the clubs had recruited younger flesh in her place? Would she become another Sandra, hard-bitten and cynical? Is that what would have happened to Tracy if she had lived? He hoped Martine at least would find someone who could love her as she deserved. She would be worth much, he thought, to the right man.

The Logan Hotel was dark except for the single light over the reception desk. Alec let Jayne in with his key, and they lingered awkwardly on the steps.

'I won't disturb Miss Helston,' Jayne said. 'I'll be all right.'

'Make sure you are. I'll see you in the morning.'

'It is morning.' In the shadow he could just see her smile, but her voice was weary. He squeezed her arm and turned to go, and heard her call good night before the lobby doors swished to behind him.

THE END